BILL FOORD

---◆---

SHERIFF SULLY'S REVENGE

Complete and Unabridged

LINFORD
Leicester

First published in Great Britain in 1995 by
Robert Hale Limited
London

First Linford Edition
published 2001
by arrangement with
Robert Hale Limited
London

British Library CIP Data

Foord, W. S. (William Spencer)
    Sheriff Sully's revenge.—Large print ed.—
Linford western library
    1. Western stories
    2. Large type books
    I. Title
    823.9'14 [F]

ISBN 0–7089–5968–7

Published by
F. A. Thorpe (Publishing)
Anstey, Leicestershire

Set by Words & Graphics Ltd.
Anstey, Leicestershire
Printed and bound in Great Britain by
T. J. International Ltd., Padstow, Cornwall

This book is printed on acid-free paper

SHERIFF SULLY'S REVENGE

When the stage-coach arrived in Hometown, each of its travellers was exhausted. They could never have envisaged how their paths would cross again and again. But how would the rugged Chip Ross figure in the struggle against his friends the Crow Indians?

There would be a bloody massacre involving the tribe and the cavalry, and Chip and Sam Cotter, an able English horseman, would find their skills and courage tested to the limit before Sheriff Sully would spring his revenge on them.

Books by Bill Foord
in the Linford Western Library:

DEATH MARCH IN MONTANA

1

The jingling and clanking of the horses' heavy harness and the grating of the coach wheels, slowing to a halt outside the stage stop, echoed across the desolate territory of the West. The noonday heat shimmered around the dusty carriage of the overland stage, trapping it in a pale yellow cloud filled with buzzing insects. The destination of the stage-coach, daubed in gold letters, Independence-St Joseph's-Hometown, were almost indistinct after gathering the dust from the trail after six hours of gruelling travel.

Hank Jackson, brown as a chestnut, the white-bearded old-timer who drove the coach, tossed the reins forward on to the backs of the horses and slotted the long whip he held. His young partner, Jem Holt, riding shot-gun, tilted his embroidered sombrero to the back of his head and wiped the sweat from his brow with the sleeve of his cotton shirt.

'One hour stop, folks,' Hank sang out to his passengers.

Before anyone could alight there was a bustle of activity from the crudely built shack, that served as a rest room, restaurant and bar. Tam and Dick Brookes, the station hands who resided in the place all the year round, darted into the open and, after a curt greeting to the driver and his partner, busied themselves with the team of six horses, weary and lathered in white sweat. The scruffy, roughneck brothers unharnessed the horses and led them to the spacious corral at the rear of the station, gave them a brisk rub down and refreshed the horses with a feed of hay and water to drink. Then, leaving the tired horses to roll and lay down in the straw bed of the corral, the station hands drove six fresh, replacement horses out of the corral and harnessed them to the coach for the last stages of the journey. Then they ambled into the shack, curious to see who were the passengers.

Rarely did they play host to such a mixed bag. Three men and a girl, and what a girl! Auburn hair in ringlets danced on her smooth forehead. She glowed with a pink, baby-faced complexion and her large eyes were a vivid blue. She was inclined to be buxom, but it suited her in a long, white silk dress. She was warm and friendly, immediately introducing herself to the coarse brothers. 'Hello, boys. I'm Dee Miller. Can you direct me to the washroom?'

While the small, plump Chinese cook served food on tin plates and laid them out on the dark, grubby kitchen-table, Tam and Dick fell over themselves to carry hot water into the washroom. The three male passengers watched Dee vanish through a door at the rear of the shack. They were so diverse in character and class, few words had passed between them during the journey, but one thing they did have in common was an admiration for the lovely young woman.

Sam Cotter, dressed in seaman's black woollen gear and carrying his worldly possessions in a small canvas kitbag failed to keep his eyes off of the beauty and he felt cocky because Dee seemed to trust him more than the other two. A warm smile from her at the start of the uncomfortable journey had broken the ice, and although the rattling and shaking of the coach was too noisy for a proper conversation to be carried on, they had exchanged a few details between them. His bold roving eye for a pretty girl had got him into trouble before and now in this strange, new country he had the common sense to act cautiously when it came to employing his handsome features and rugged charm to attract female strangers. 'Dee sings for a living,' he announced, showing off his advance knowledge of her.

Hank Jackson, the coach driver,

wiped bean juice from his silver beard and looked down the long table at young Sam. 'I'm local born and bred in Hometown. Maybe there's things you ought to know about Miss Miller.'

'I don't mean to step on anyone's toes,' Sam said.

'Dee was as popular on the stage at The Centre in Hometown as any gal I ever did see. Lovely voice and pretty as a picture, but she wanted to be a star, so she hopped off to New Orleans. She upset quite a few folks by quitting Hometown.'

'So I can imagine.'

A thin, boyish character with mean eyes and a pale complexion, dressed in the fashion of a gunfighter, smirked at Sam's precise reply. He carried a pair of Colt .45 revolvers slung from a thick, leather belt. His battered Stetson hat was tipped low over his face and he wore a grubby white shirt with a black lace tie. His blue, cotton jacket was unbuttoned and his trousers were made of rough tweed. His heavy boots ensured he made a lot of noise when he walked. He'd wolfed back his food with large spoonfuls that cleared his plate in six rapid scoops, and now he pushed back his chair to give him room to twirl his guns and rehearse his fast-drawing.

'What sort of fancy talk is that, kid?'

'I'm sorry, I suppose I do sound rather quaint. I'm English.'

'You don't say!'

'From a rather smart town named Lewes in the county of Sussex. It is quite well known for horse-riding.'

'Yeah, well, I'm Ben Wild from Chicago. The toughest city in the world where you have to back up your words with deeds. I've been a hungry slum kid all my life, but I've heard there's a fortune to be made by anyone who can shoot straight and fast.'

The third passenger, who had been picking at his food, suddenly took an interest in young Ben Wild. He was too fat for comfort with a round, moon face as flabby as a pig's and matching thick lips and tiny eyes. His expensive suit was city-made. Everything about Hoot Clackson was pompous, ruthless and greedy. He owned Townend, the largest ranch between Independence and Hometown, but wouldn't be satisfied till he owned all the plains that linked the growing towns on the Missouri.

'You can earn a fortune, young man, if you survive,' he told Ben.

'There be ten tombstones in a Chicago cemetery that'll tell you if I've survived,' Ben boasted.

His outrageous claim silenced the rest of them at the table and they stopped eating and stared at him in awe. Ben never smiled and he showed his satisfaction of spreading fear among them by a cynical curl of his thin lips.

After a long pause, old-timer Hank, who'd seen pretty well everything in the Wild West likely to shock any law-abiding citizen, said icily, 'I'd never have taken you on board if I'd known you were a gunfighter.'

'Don't fret, Grandpa. You'll all be safe providing nobody upsets me.'

Jem Holt was considered a marksman by the stage-coach company and he rode shot-gun because he despised all villains. Ben's arrogance alone was sufficient to make him disliked on sight. 'That's some reputation you are carrying. It's a gunfighter's reputation that puts the fear of the devil into ordinary folk, long before he hits their town.'

'Yeah, well, just you believe it, I've got that reputation.'

Hank quickly switched the conversation before he called the kid a lying braggart and he turned to Sam. 'What's a sailor doing heading West?'

Sam grinned pleasantly and managed to ease the tension in the room. 'I'm no sailor, Hank, I just worked my passage from England as a deck hand on a schooner.'

Hank took stock of the young man's handsome features, his complexion weatherbeaten from the rough living before the mast. His hands too were strong and scarred. 'Must have been hard on you, Sam. Why did you do it?'

Sam shrugged. He was tall and wiry and Hank suspected he was a strong, rugged lad even before his gruelling experiences aboard the ship crossing the Atlantic.

'I lost my job.'

'What's your line, Sam?'

'Horses. They be the only thing I know about. Breaking, riding, grooming and all that.'

'You told us your town was horse country. Why come to America?'

'It's big and spacious. The wide-open plains appeal to me and I reckon anyone who can handle a horse won't starve.'

'Would you have starved back in England?' persisted Hank.

Sam pushed away his empty plate and he caught Hank with a mischievous gleam in his eyes. 'I was Lord Stonegate's head stable-boy and jockey. Over the jumps, y'know. I won a lot of races and a lot of friends. His pretty niece was among them.'

Hank groaned. 'I got the feeling there

was a gal behind it all.'

'She did the chasing, honest! Estate manager caught us in a hay-loft. I got a flogging, the sack and no references, and that's why I'm here, penniless and without a job.'

'They are taking on dashing young riders for the Pony Express,' Hank advised him.

'Pony Express? What's that?'

'In short, taking mail and documents from Missouri to California. It means riding hell-for-leather in relays to deliver the mail in ten days. There's going to be a starting point in Hometown. You ought to apply.'

Sam was about to thank Hank for tipping him off when Hoot Clackson broke in rudely, 'Moonshine! Pie-in-the-sky. If it ever gets off the ground, the Pony Express won't last.'

'What makes you say that?' asked Sam.

'Because I've been out East talking turkey to the people who are going to build a railway right across the country, and they want my land. It'll be the railway that's going to carry the freight, the passengers and the mail.'

Hoot calmly lit a fat cigar and blew smoke into the air, where it drifted along the table. Sam decided his arrogance was equal to that of Ben Wild's and it roused old Hank's anger. 'Say, Mr Clackson, if you sell them rail guys all your land it'll kill off the need for horses. We won't need stage-coaches or even cowboys to drive the herds to market.'

'Good thinking, old man. The iron horse will carry the cattle.'

'It ain't to our liking,' retorted Hank.

He quit the table as if he no longer accepted the company he was in. Jem and Sam followed him and the trio sat at the makeshift bar and ordered beers. Sam thought it curious that Clackson and Ben Wild had moved close together and were engaged in an earnest conversation, but he paid scant attention to them because Dee emerged from the wash-room, hair freshly groomed and complexion sparkling. She winked at Sam and asked, 'How's the chow?'

'Pretty fair, better than ship's biscuits and weevil.'

The Chinese cook laid a meal before her at the long table and somehow produced a clean napkin, but after a few minutes of eating, Dee looked displeased. The radiance deserted her features and her eyes were clouded. It was only when Hank announced the hour's stop was up and the coach was due to roll that the young woman seemed comfortable again. As the crew and passengers filed out of the shack, Dee reached out and pulled Sam back.

'Sam, can I trust you?'

'I'd like to think so.'

'Those two, the fat dude and the skinny kid with the gun.'

'What about them?'

'Fifty dollars changed hands.'

'Paying a gunfighter fifty dollars usually means one thing, Dee.'

'You catch on quickly the ways of the

West, Sam,' she said, raising her fine eyebrows.

'Ben Wild and Clackson were discussing the fortune a gunfighter could make out here.'

'Did they mention any names?'

'Not while I was at the table.'

'My hearing is very keen, Sam.'

They were outdoors now and the sun blazed down from a clear sky, bouncing off the stationary stage-coach and dazzling the passengers as they climbed aboard. Sam squinted down at Dee. 'Tell me, what did you hear?'

'Clackson has hired Ben Wild to kill Chip Ross,' her voice trembled as she choked out the words.

Sam looked blank and didn't know how to reply. Hank and Jem were up front of the stage-coach. 'Don't hang about down there,' Hank shouted impatiently.

'I don't know who Chip Ross might be,' Sam said weakly.

'He's the man I've come back to Hometown for. There's no more time to talk now. We'll meet at the end of the journey and I'll explain everything.'

They climbed into the coach to join the arrogant gunfighter and the wealthy landowner.

2

The heat in the afternoon was stifling inside the coach, and together with the uncomfortable bouncing of the vehicle and the boring scenery of endless, arid plains, the journey was almost intolerable. The filling of the air with Hoot Clackson's vile cigar smoke didn't help either. Sam and Dee managed to stay patient, but the conditions irked Ben Wild to such an extent he became truculent and his mood was cynical as he amused himself by teasing Dee in an aggressive manner. 'Entertainer, are you?' he said, laughing scornfully. 'That's what they call a certain type of woman in Chicago.'

Dee blushed with embarrassment and turned her head to avoid looking at the arrogant youth, but Ben refused to stop his taunting and the sips of whisky he stole from the hip flask heightened his defiance and slurred his words. 'I'm talking to you,' he snarled.

The desolate plains bordering a wilderness of shrubland sped past. Sam shared Dee's pretence of an interest in the dull landscape and they conversed in whispers. Ben hated to be ignored and the reputation he'd created for himself gave him a top-dog feeling. The liquor had gone to his head and put a scarlet flush to his pale, seedy face. His anger had risen and he felt reckless. Hoot Clackson, seated beside the youth fidgeted in discomfort but, as he considered he was the gunfighter's employer after commissioning him for a killing, he said quietly, 'Don't be a nuisance, lad.'

'I only asked a question. Ain't she got the manners to answer?'

'He's a born troublemaker,' Sam whispered, 'best humour him.'

'If it'll shut him up,' sighed Dee.

'What you two whispering about, eh?' Ben demanded.

'I'm a singer and nothing else,' Dee told him firmly.

'What! And you work in the saloons?'

'That doesn't make me what you are suggesting.'

'If you sang so prettily why did you quit New Orleans?'

The taunt hit Dee on a raw spot. It was as if Ben knew the truth and was testing her out and she found it impossible to be frank with him. Sam frowned at her and offered her a brief, warning shake of his head, and it was up to Dee to think quickly and silence Ben. Her eyes flashed defiantly at him as she swung round to stare at him. 'If you must know, I was a flop in New Orleans and after I was hissed off the stage a few times, I decided I'd rather be a big fish in a little pond like Hometown. That's why I've come back. Satisfied?'

There was nothing more for Ben to say to satisfy his teasing. Dee had admitted she'd never be a star in the big city and it foxed Ben because the girl was so humble. He grunted and sat hunched in the corner of the coach staring out of the window. Presently he embarked on another topic to make an impression. 'Say, where are all these redskins I hear about? Ain't they supposed to be savage?'

'Some are, some are friendly,' Hoot told him.

'I reckon they'll be all the same to me,' Ben said, patting his guns.

Sam feared what he heard. 'What do you mean?'

'I mean if I spot any guys that ain't got pale faces then I'll pick a few off just to keep my hand in.'

'They are not wild animals,' Dee snapped at him.

Ben laughed at her, drew his revolvers and checked they were loaded, then gave a display of fast-drawing before restoring the guns to their holsters. He searched the faces of the other passengers to see if they registered astonishment at his skill. Only Hoot derived any pleasure from the display. Dee shivered with unpleasant visions, while Sam wondered how he'd come to ride with such an uncouth villain.

It was late in the afternoon when a movement in the undergrowth gave some variety to the boring journey. A herd of wild pigs rushed out of the long, dry grass, apparently disturbed by the noisy rattle and crossed the stage-trail. Ben grew excited and leaned out of the coach window. 'Anyone fancy roast pork for dinner?' he asked, drawing both guns.

The herd scampered and jostled to the far side of the track, but when a shrill whistling and enthusiastic yelling echoed in the wild pigs' wake, the situation became more tense. A trio of Indians, riding piebald ponies and armed with short spears and bows and arrows swooped out of the tall under-growth to hunt down their prey.

'Whoopee!' cried Ben. 'What have we here?'

He aimed his guns but, before he

could shoot, Clackson, acting more responsibly than he had previously, said in alarm, 'Don't you dare shoot.'

Sam jumped to his feet, rigid with anger; both his fists were clenched and it seemed nothing would stop him pouncing on the reckless Ben.

'They are redskins, ain't they?' retorted Ben, glaring at Hoot.

'Cherokee,' snapped Hoot.

'What does that mean?'

'It shows how green you are to the West,' Dee interrupted.

'Put those guns away. The Cherokee are peaceful, hard-working farmers and friendly too,' Hoot rapped.

'Aw, just one less won't matter.'

The hunting party ignored the stage-coach as the Indians crossed the trail and gave chase. They were now out of sight from Ben's side of the coach and he lurched towards the side where Sam and Dee sat, but Sam blocked his passage to the window. The two young men became locked in a close encounter and neither was prepared to give way.

'I want to get at that window,' Ben snarled.

'Get back to your seat,' ordered Sam.

'I'm after bagging myself my first redskin, and you ain't going to stop me.'

Sam didn't hesitate although the customs of the West were foreign to him. At present, Indian tribes were all the same to him and maybe it was common practice to shoot on sight any redskin, but it just seemed wrong to him to kill any human being in cold blood. He fixed Ben with a cool stare and without giving away his intentions he brought his right fist up from his hip in a fierce uppercut. It landed squarely on Ben's chin, lifting him off his feet and laying him out in Hoot Clackson's lap, but in the swift process of denying the young gunman access to the window, Ben's revolvers fired two shots that burst through the coach ceiling.

Hoot Clackson gaped in astonishment at the ease with which Sam had dealt with Ben, and Sam's coolness was quite unnerving to the wealthy land-owner who had thought he'd hired a skilled gunfighter on the cheap. The two shots had come close to singeing his eyebrows and while Dee had uttered a frightened squeal it was Hank Jackson, in charge of the team of horses, who reacted venomously.

The coach skidded to a standstill, rocking the occupants to and fro, and Hank climbed to the ground, a pistol clenched in his fist. He threw open the coach door, his eyes blazing, not knowing where to look first.

'What in damnation is going on?'

Nobody spoke for a moment and Hank sniffed at the cordite that circled Ben's face in a grey cloud and scowled at the revolvers that were held in his limp hands. 'All of you lost your tongues, eh? Well, I don't reckon to have guns going off in my stage-coach, especially when the bullets almost went through my beard. Now, do I get an answer or do I turf you out of here and let you walk the rest of the way to Hometown?'

Hoot pushed Ben's prone body off his lap and he landed on the floor with a bump and a groan, which failed to bring him round. 'The guns went off by accident,' he explained weakly.

'I hit Ben,' Sam confessed.

Hank took a close look at the stunned man on the floor and then gave Sam a questioning glance. 'What they call you at home, son? Hammerfist?'

Sam shrugged and admitted boxing was a noble art where he came from. 'I also had to deal with a bullying bosun on the voyage over,' he added.

Hank looked past Sam and said to Dee, 'Well, young lady, you haven't said anything yet?'

'That thug wanted to shoot at the Cherokee hunting party just for target practice,' she said, nodding resentfully at Ben.

'The Cheokee tribe along this trail are my friends,' declared Hank. 'I'll make sure we'll have no more nonsense.'

He removed the guns from Ben's hands. 'He can have these back at the end of the trip. Now p'raps we can get going.'

Hank returned to the driver's seat and the coach moved slowly forward before the horses broke into a gallop. It was another minute and with nobody showing any concern for the unconscious Ben, before the young man crawled on to a seat. He nursed a swollen jaw and his head ached. He only once glared at Sam, but his mouth seemed paralysed to issue threats and, when he discovered his guns were missing, he decided to remain silent anyhow.

Hoot glanced angrily at him and whispered, 'You'll have to do better than what I've just seen, or I'll take back my dollars.'

Ben grunted an irritable reply and for the rest of the journey he sat sulking in the corner of the coach.

Hometown was being bathed in a red sunset by the time the stage-coach rumbled along the dusty main street. The stores that faced each other were locked up and shuttered with stout timber boards. A sole horseman was riding out of town, three cowboys dressed in their best gear were hitching their horses to a post and when Hank pulled up his team of horses outside the well-lit, vulgarly decorated Centre Hometown's bawdy establishment, that provided heavy gambling, wine, women and song, the arrival of the stage-coach went almost ignored.

'Far as we go, folks,' Hank sang out to his passengers.

Somehow his cracked, raucous voice penetrated the bar and gambling tables of the Centre and a horde of people stampeded through the swing doors to see who had arrived.

Luggage was dumped on the side-walk. Dee's arrival was greeted with frantic cheering and crude whistling and she took the welcome home from the townsfolk who remembered her before she took off for New Orleans with a cheerful smile. Then suddenly it was as if a dark cloud had descended over the town. The laughter, ribald remarks and saucy whistles that welcomed Dee were cut dead as the swaggering, burly figure of Sheriff Rick Sully pushed open the swing doors of the saloon and strutted through the crowd. When he'd reached the front he stood with short legs astride and podgy hands on his hips; his eyes flat as glass gleamed out of his scarred, cruel face. He was on the small side, but tough and ruthless and although he'd brought law and order to the growing, rambling Hometown, his bullying methods had not won him the respect of the people. He'd turned the place from a lawless town into a sad and corrupt one and if he'd gained recognition as a good lawman it was only because he could handle villains from his wide experience of being one himself. He enjoyed running the town. It was easier and less risky than cattle-rustling, robbing banks or gun-fighting, and he had the backing of the wealthy ranchers and landowners, while his sidekick, Deputy Poker Dines, some reckoned was nastier than the sheriff.

Rick Sully studied the passengers who'd alighted from the coach. He gave a thin smile of approval to Hoot Clackson and although the landowner had done most of the fixing to appoint Sully as the town's feared lawman, the sheriff was too independent to be servile to anyone.

Hoot Clackson nodded in recognition and, when a couple of lackeys from the saloon appeared to carry his pieces of luggage up to the room he'd booked for the night, the landowner quickly vanished from the scene.

Dee and Sam came under Sully's relentless scrutiny, however. Sam felt uneasy with those flat eyes running the rule over him and when the lawman spoke he had a cynical drawl. 'I like to get a good look at any stranger coming into my town, and if I don't like what I see they get moved on.'

'I am no stranger,' said Dee, her spirited reply bringing a bright pink colour to her cheeks. 'Everyone in Hometown knows me. You are the stranger!'

'Maybe, we ain't met before now, but I've heard about you, Miss Miller. You'll find changes here since I replaced old man Thorn. Who is your sailor friend?'

Sam Cotter introduced himself and added hotly, 'I'm not a sailor, I just dressed like this for the voyage from England.'

'What the hell you doing in Hometown?'

'Looking for a job.'

'Reckoning on staying, eh?'

'I hope so.'

Rick Sully squinted at him. 'There ain't no room for saddle-tramps or hangers-on in my town. I'll be keeping an eye on you, boy. You can beat it for now.'

Sam ushered Dee through the crowd into the saloon. 'What sort of snake is he?'

Dee paused at the threshold of the smoke-filled saloon and looked enquiringly into Sam's face. 'I wanted to report to the sheriff what I overheard between Ben Wild and Clackson at the stage-stop.'

'He's busy right now,' Sam observed, glancing over his shoulder.

Rick Sully's alertness never missed anything and when he caught Hank discreetly returning the pair of revolvers he'd taken from Ben Wild, the sheriff intervened with the swiftness of a swooping bird. Ben hardly had time to lower the revolvers into his holsters before Sully was on to him, his strong hands closing round Ben's wrists and looking meanly at the young gunman. 'I'll take care of your firearms, boy.'

Ben, who felt undressed without his guns, swore violently at the lawman. 'It's a man's right to carry his guns!'

'Not in my town, except for me and my deputy. We're the only men to do any shooting, everyone else hands in their weapons between sunset and sunrise.'

'What if I refuse?'

'Then you move straight out of Hometown, pronto.'

Rick Sully wasted no more time on the rebellious youth. He took the revolvers from him and told Ben to collect them from the sheriff's office in the morning. Ben pushed past the tough lawman, muttering a boastful threat and headed for the bar in the saloon.

Sam watched the short, ugly incident break up. 'Ben Wild will do no killing tonight.'

'I'm still determined to report what I overheard to the sheriff. Will you come with me, Sam?'

They moved into the saloon and found a small table for two just as the crowd dispersed from outside and filled the place. A waiter paused as he filled a tray with empty glasses. 'What you drinking?' he asked.

Sam looked embarrassed and Dee

stepped in and ordered two small beers.

'I'm sorry I've only a couple of dimes to my name till I land a job,' he apologized.

'Where will you sleep tonight?'

Sam took stock of the plush surroundings of the establishment, owned by a powerful syndicate of ranchers. 'Not here, that's for sure.'

'I guess that means you'll sleep rough.'

'Good guess,' smiled Sam.

She closed her warm hand over Sam's. 'Will you be here in the morning?'

'To go with you to see the sheriff?'

She nodded eagerly. 'You can tell him what a crazy kid Ben Wild is.'

Sam didn't jump at the suggestion even when he took into account how it might advance his relationship with the lovely girl. He realized he'd impressed her by taking a defiant stand against Ben during the long journey to Hometown. He also knew why she'd given up a chance of fame in New

Orleans. Her yearning for a man named Chip Ross must be desperate so Sam wasn't keen to become involved with another man's woman. Pretty girls had caused him trouble on several occasions during his twenty years and he wasn't even at home in this new country.

Dee was quick to notice his reluctance. She smiled sweetly and told him, 'I don't know of anyone else to trust.'

'But you are well known in this town?'

'Sam, if I asked anyone for a favour, can't you guess what they'd suggest in return? Look, if I can't depend on you, then I'll ride out to Chip's place and warn him that a gunman's been hired to kill him.'

Sam frowned at her. She was strong, self-willed and determined and he put it to her that was the quickest and most sensible solution to the problem. She sighed in despair and the expression in her eyes suggested she'd almost given up on him. 'You don't understand,' she said crossly.

'I might if you took me into your confidence.'

'Chip's spread is twenty miles from here. It stands in the centre of Camp Waterfall. Hoot Clackson owns all the land to the south, but the north . . . '

She lowered her voice and looked grave. Sam noticed her hands trembled nervously. He suddenly felt he was being drawn into an involvement with her without volunteering. 'What about the north of this Camp Waterfall?'

'It's all Crow country.'

Sam shrugged. 'I'm green to this land. What does that mean?'

'The Crow tribe are as savage a fighting race as you'll come against. Chip manages to keep them friendly with him because he supplies them with a special breed of pony. That's what Chip does, breeds and trades in horses.'

Sam looked more interested in Dee's request. Any man who bred horses was a kindred spirit and he suddenly wanted to meet Chip Ross, but why would anyone want him killed? Sam wasn't going to stick his neck out without being denied all the facts. He drank the glass of beer and leaned back in his chair watching Dee take sips from her glass.

'Have you made up your mind?' Dee asked.

'We'll go and talk to the sheriff first thing in the morning. He doesn't appear to be a man to cross, but if he won't do anything about Hoot and Ben, then we'll ride out to Camp Waterfall, although I can't fathom why a horse-trader is in the way of his neighbour.'

'Folk call Chip an Indian-lover. Hoot Clackson hates the Crow tribe and he has a running feud with Chip over the water-rights. A wide river flows along the centre of the land owned by Chip.'

'Phew! And that's enough to have a bloke killed? What sort of country is this?'

'It's the way of the West, Sam. See you outside this saloon in the morning,' she said, climbing to her feet.

Sam stood up politely and watched

her go upstairs to her room. Before he sat down again, a slim man of more than six foot, wearing the badge of a deputy, sidled up to him. Sam disliked the lawman on sight. His narrow features and cunning eyes seemed to suit a character who played second fiddle to Rick Sully. 'That dame's too snooty for the likes of you, stranger,' he said.

'And who might you be to select my friends?' Sam's indignant retort brought a look of surprise on the deputy's face.

'I'll tell you who I am. The name's Poker Dines, and I carry a lot of weight in this town. You might say, between us, me and Rick run Hometown.'

'I see,' nodded Sam. 'I've already met the sheriff.'

'Now, if you'd like a swell dame who'd make you comfortable for the night, I can introduce you to one for a small fee.'

'You mean you're a pimp?'

Poker Dines slapped the holster that housed his Colt revolver as a warning gesture. 'Don't call me that. I hate the word. I can just be helpful to strangers, but if they upset me, I'll see them booted out of town as soon as look at them.'

'I'll remember that.'

Sam eased his way past the deputy and out of the saloon, where the heavy gambling and drinking was in full swing. He strode along the dark street, his kitbag over his shoulder till he came to a livery stable that was empty and up for sale. He sneaked into the premises through a side-door that was loose on its hinges and sank to the floor, his weary body scuffling the thin layer of musty straw. He spread out his blanket and was soon asleep.

At first light, the sun streaked through the gaps in the timber-clad stable, but it was a hefty kick in the ribs that awoke Sam. He sat up, roaring an oath at his assailant and recognized the bullying frame of Rick Sully.

'I reckon I figured you about right the first time I laid eyes on you,' growled the sheriff, 'we got no room for scroungers and loafers in this town.'

Sully grabbed Sam by the neck and hauled him to his feet. The lawman was immensely strong despite his short, fat figure and his hands were like steel.

'What harm am I doing, Sheriff?'

'You broke in.'

'For a night's sleep.'

'That's what I mean. A useless loafer.'

'I haven't a dime to my name, that's true, but I'll do anything to earn a few dollars.'

'Then do it someplace else. Clear out of Hometown or I'll clap you in jail.'

'Give me a break. I'm meeting Miss Miller this morning . . . '

The popularity of the singer was enough for Sully to mellow his anger, and he was forced to take into account the respect Dee had always commanded in the town. He narrowed his eyes and looked suspiciously at Sam. 'Say, what is it between you and the saloon singer?'

'We just got friendly on the stage-coach journey,' Sam shrugged.

'Why you, when she brushed off every man in Hometown?'

'She says she trusts me.'

'What does she have to trust you over?'

'There are things she doesn't feel she wants to do alone.'

'Like what?'

'Discussing something she overheard between Hoot Clackson and that crazy kid Ben Wild. We were coming to see you.'

Sam couldn't be certain if it was the name of Hoot Clackson or of Ben Wild that caused the abrupt change in Sully's pugnacious expression.

'Is it something I ought to know about?' questioned the sheriff. He gave his best imitation of a friendly smile he could muster and he laid his powerful hand upon Sam's shoulder, but Sam sensed he was impatient for a reply.

'Well, I guess it'll save me and Miss Miller coming to your office.'

'Sure will. The place gets crowded each morning when we're issuing the cowboys with their guns we confiscated last evening.'

'It was at the last stage-stop on the journey here. Hoot and Ben Wild had their heads together, sitting at the same table where Dee was eating her meal.'

'Forget the details. You said she overheard something. Important was it?'

'Hoot handed Ben fifty dollars.'

'What for?'

'He's hired him to kill a man named Chip Ross.'

Sully's bloated face went blank for a moment, then he threw back his head and roared helplessly with laughter. His mouth opened so wide it almost caused his mean, little eyes to shut and he slapped Sam on the back so heartily it nearly sent the young man sprawling.

'Have I said something funny?' asked Sam.

'Funniest thing I've ever heard.'

'Dee is very devoted to Chip I understand.'

'Maybe, maybe,' said Sully, his laughter reduced to a scornful chuckle. 'Chip Ross ain't liked in Hometown on account of him being an Indian-lover. He employs the Crow scum on round-ups and on the trail rather than give decent cowboys work. I'd say there's scores of men who'd like to have a shot, but Hoot Clackson isn't one of them.'

'Then, you don't believe what Dee claims she heard?'

'Not in a month of Sundays. Just forget it, kid.'

'I can't forget it. Dee's determined to ride out and warn Chip.'

3

Rick Sully suddenly forgot about his threat to order Sam to leave town and he left the empty livery stables in a hurry, although trying to disguise the fact that he was perturbed by Sam's disclosure. He strutted along the deserted main street till he reached the Centre and hammered on the locked doors of the local place of entertainment.

'Clear off,' yelled someone inside, 'we don't open till noon.'

'Open up. Sheriff Sully here.'

He was obeyed instantly. A little, bent man wearing a white apron over his suit and brandishing a broom, drew the bolts on the swing doors. Sully barged past him. The odour of stale beer and acrid smoke hit him in the face as he crossed the floor of the saloon ankle-deep in litter. The gambling tables remained whisky-stained with decks of cards strewn across them, just as they were left at closing-time the previous night.

Sully climbed the stairs that led to the hotel rooms and knew where to find Hoot Clackson. He thumped on the door of the best room in the place, turned the knob and burst in without being invited. Hoot was sitting at a small table, dressed in an outsized, golden dressing-gown, poring over a sheaf of business papers. He widened his eyes and jumped to his feet, startled at the rude intrusion, but Sully charged across the room, livid with anger.

'What the devil do you mean by flying in here like an enraged hornet?' demanded Hoot.

'You should keep your door locked.'

'I'm waiting for my breakfast to be served.'

Sully sank into a velvet-covered chair. 'Are you double-crossing me?'

'What a strange notion, Rick. Have you just awoke from a bad dream?'

'I ain't dreamt that you paid that

crazy kid Ben Wild fifty dollars to kill Chip Ross. What's your game?'

Hoot threw down his gold fountain-pen and sighed irritably. He regarded Sully carefully, having no desire to upset him for many reasons. Sully had been a notorious outlaw, but had changed sides when the subtle Hoot recognized his ability to be the best man to clear up the lawless, growing town. Sully's terms were hard. A fat salary and he chose his own deputy, the lecherous, evil Poker Dines. They ran the girls in the upstairs rooms and took a ten per cent levy off all the gambling winnings, but there were worse arrangements which only Hoot and the two lawmen knew about. It was the reason why Hoot handled the sheriff as if he was a keg of dynamite. If Sully opened his mouth and spoke out of turn, the locals who were ruled by fear would riot and tear the town apart and probably end up lynching him. 'Who has let the cat out of the bag?' he snapped.

'Then you admit it?'

'Damn it, Rick, we keep no secrets from each other. I was going to tell you.'

'Yeah, I bet.'

He leaned forward and helped himself to one of Hoot's fat, expensive cigars lying in an open case on the small table. He lit it and blew a cloud of smoke towards the uncomfortable land-owner.

'I have much to tell you in fact.'

'Well, shoot! I'm listening.'

'In the next few days we'll be needing an extra gun.'

'What makes you think this Ben Wild is any good?'

'I don't, except he's dead keen to earn a living as a professional gun-fighter. He's determined and arrogant and a hungry boy from the slums of Chicago.'

'You reckon that makes a gunfighter, eh?'

'It was worth fifty dollars to give him a chance.'

'Sounds more like you are undercutting me and Poker. We've always been your hired gunmen, but assassinations ain't never as cheap as fifty dollars, especially when innocent men bite the dust.'

'Don't think I've forgotten what your going rate is, Rick. I pay you and Poker five times what I paid young Wild but, as I said before, we may need an extra gun. Things are going to happen in this county, very soon.'

'Oh, yeah and were you going to tell me about them, too?'

'Sure I was. Haven't I just spent a week in the East talking to the railway surveyors and St Joseph's and ending up in California? It's progress and exciting, Rick.'

'And it's cutting across your land. I've heard the railway people are paying a fortune for land.'

'Is just happens to be the best route,' Hoot said absently.

'But you don't own all the land.'

'Not yet.'

The two men exchanged cunning glances. Hoot selected a cigar from his case, lit it and smoked with obvious pleasure while his comment was carefully considered by the sheriff.

'I ain't no fool,' said Sully, 'I got an inkling what you're getting at. Do you think it'll be that simple?'

'I've spoken to people in high places,' boasted Hoot. 'There's a hundred United States Cavalry on the way. They'll be based at Hometown till I give word to clear those Crow squatters from Camp Waterfall.'

'That sounds like trouble. The Crow are savage fighters.'

'There are but twenty families who have set up a lodge on that land. They have no right to be there. They are a northern tribe who followed the migrating buffalo herds, but found they liked the climate here and have put down roots.'

'And when their lodge is wiped out, you move in and buy the land for next to nothing.'

'No trouble at all. The Crow will be vastly outnumbered.'

'You're talking about slaughter. I got no love for the redskins, but they 'ave given no trouble since settling at Camp Waterfall.'

'Are you getting squeamish, Rick? That comes from having a peaceful job since you've cleaned up Hometown?'

'All I'm saying is nobody has to be killed and cause an Indian uprising. Give the tribe twenty-four hours to move on.'

Hoot chewed over the suggestion. His stomach rumbled and he looked hopefully at the door for the waiter to bring him his breakfast on a tray. He loved the huge plateful of ham and eggs the hotel dished out, but Rick Sully's presence, especially his objection to the scheme already worked out between him, the military and the government was upsetting his digestion. 'You need a good reason to move the Crow tribe out of their lodge.'

'I'll find one. Illegal trading of guns

and whisky. It'll have to be a frame-up and Nickel Joe, the Indian trader will have to be arrested, but it should be enough to frighten the Crow people to pack up and leave.'

'And who is going to warn them?'

'Me and Poker will round up a posse.'

'You mean, bring that gang of outlaws into Hometown? They scare the folk here.'

'Better than have Indian raids start up all over the county.'

Hoot sighed miserably, but couldn't deny that Rick Sully always handled difficult situations cleverly and efficiently. 'All right, do it your way. It's going to take a day for the cavalry to reach Hometown, but you make sure your mob of cut-throats quit this town immediately after your job is done.'

Hoot was satisfied all the loose ends were now secure and he decided to extend his stay at the hotel for a few more days. Camp Waterfall was going to be a chaotic place while the Crow tribe were chased out of their lodge and if he was absent from his ranch nobody could point an accusing finger at him. He waited for Sully to get up and go about his daily business, but the sheriff was in no hurry. He screwed the butt of his cigar into an ashtray, sat back comfortably in the plush chair and tilted his wide-brimmed hat to the back of his head. Hoot was worried; he wasn't expecting to share his breakfast with the man.

'You claimed someone had let the cat out of the bag,' Sully reminded the scheming landowner.

'I don't reckon that's important now.'

'Shooting down Chip Ross is the most important thing in this set-up.'

'I've told Ben Wild I don't care how it's done as long as Ross is dead within the next couple of days. I'm hoping a bullet in the back will get rid of that stubborn Indian-lover.'

'That ain't going to happen.'

'What do you mean!'

'Sam Cotter spilled the beans to me

an hour ago. Dee Miller wants me to do something about you hiring Ben Wild to shoot Chip.'

Hoot's eyes bolted and his fat lips twitched nervously. 'Damn!'

'Don't fret. I've reassured young Cotter you're the nicest guy in the county.'

'Thanks, Rick. What that gal overheard might have ruined the whole scheme.'

'It may still have.'

'What! You sit there as cold as ice . . . '

'Listen. The fact I'm doing nothing to stop Ben Wild ain't the end of the matter. Sam Cotter has agreed to ride out with Dee to warn Chip, and that stubborn horse-dealer won't let himself get shot so you can buy his spread. I'd better remind you, Chip Ross draws a fast gun and one word from him can bring a score of Crow bucks to his assistance.'

'I have to get rid of him,' stormed Hoot.

'Then you know what you've got to do.'

Sully climbed to his feet, helped himself to another of Hoot's expensive cigars and strode to the door. Hoot watched him, wishing the lawman wasn't so superior. 'I know what I've got to do,' he said tersely, 'will you tell Ben Wild to get up here?'

⋆ ⋆ ⋆

Sam wasn't kept waiting more than ten minutes outside the Centre before Dee appeared. She looked sparkling and refreshing in a cowboy shirt and brown riding slacks with just a suspicion of auburn curls peeping out from an enormous sun-hat, secured under her chin by a thin strap. It seemed to Sam she intended riding out to see Chip Ross irrespective of what the outcome of a visit to the sheriff might be. Standing beside her, Sam felt like a hobo. It hadn't been possible to shave and his hair was thick and shaggy. His seaman's rig was by now worse for wear, the woolen jumper too hot for this torrid climate. Dee gave him a generous smile and didn't appear to be taken aback when Sam told her, 'It'll be a waste of time talking to the sheriff. I get the feeling he's in Clackson's pay. He won't have anything bad said about the bloke.'

'This is a corrupt town, Sam. I've been talking to a few people. Anyone who quarrels with Hoot Clackson seems to vanish.'

'What shall we do?'

'Hire a couple of horses and ride out to Camp Waterfall. I know what I heard at the stage-stop between Clackson and Ben Wild. We must warn Chip.'

A side turning off of the town's main street took them to a livery stable owned by the huge, bearded and jovial Anvil Smith. On the door of the premises was a poster advertising for young riders to enlist in the delivery of mail and document service under the title of 'Pony Express.'

Anvil greeted the lovely Dee with a bear hug. 'Nice to have you back,' he beamed.

'Hometown's changed, Anvil.'

'Sure has, maybe it ain't so wild these days, but it's more sinister, like folk have to be careful what they say. Who is your friend, Dee?'

Dee had to pull Sam away from the poster to introduce him. Sam's hand was wrung in a grip of steel, but he managed to exchange friendly smiles with the mountain of a man.

'You interested in being a Pony Express rider, Sam?'

'I need a job and I've spent my life with horses.'

'Plenty of adventure for a dashing youngster. I'm supplying the horses.'

'I'll apply when we get back from Camp Waterfall. The stage-coach offices are running the show I see.'

Anvil brought forward a pair of horses, already saddled, and when he saw the ease with which Sam leaped into the saddle of a large, powerful

Morgan, he raised his shaggy eyebrows and said, 'Aye, you do that. Tell them I sent you. I reckon you be a natural for the job.'

Dee was given a strong American Quarter Horse, the popular, fast saddle-horse and Sam was satisfied by the way she sat in the saddle; he had no need to fuss over his female companion with regard to her riding skill.

They packed provisions and plenty of water for the twenty-mile ride and set off at a gentle trot. Once out of Hometown it was a vast, empty land and only when they took to the high ground of the foothills that overlooked a wide and long valley did they see any sign of habitation.

The couple rested often, working the horses no more than five miles at a stretch. Sitting in the cool of the hills they gazed upon a scene of flat country that ran straight across the county, interlaced by the growing towns of Missouri, Independence and St Joseph. Beyond the clusters of buildings, shimmering in the heat of the day, quietly rolled the magnificent river Missouri, peaceful and still as glass.

They abandoned the hills as they grew more craggy and boulder-ridden and descended into the valley. Sam became sensitive to the desolation and because he was green to the country it was a chilling experience to ride in the shadow of the towering hills. He felt they were a marked pair, pinpointed for an attack from the cover of the ground above them, and he couldn't understand why he suffered the pangs of fear. It was instinctive to keep a watchful eye on the hills and his caution was immediately noticed by Dee.

'Is something bothering you?'

'Just staying alert.'

'Is that why we've come into the valley?'

'We don't carry guns. I haven't the dollars to arm myself, so I reckoned our best defence was a fast escape across this flat country.'

Dee thrust her hand in the back

pocket of her slacks and withdrew a miniature pistol. 'I bought this in New Orleans, especially designed for ladies.'

'Good enough for close range. Not much in a gunfight proper.'

'Do you think we're in danger of being attacked?' she asked, putting the small revolver away.

Sam pursed his lips and looked sheepish, but it made sense to confess to his companion that when he'd spoken to Sheriff Sully he was off his guard. 'I'm sorry, Dee, but I let it slip we were determined to warn Chip he was in danger.'

She reacted angrily, her large eyes gleaming in despair because of Sam's carelessness. 'Of all the people to tell!' she cried.

'How was I to know Sully's a crooked lawman?'

'Crooked or honest, you shouldn't have told him we intended to ride out to Camp Waterfall.'

'I have to admit, Dee, I've got this feeling we're being shadowed.'

'Just a feeling is it? I'll wager a hundred dollars there's someone watching us from the hills.'

'And he'll stop us reaching Chip?'

'That's pretty obvious. If Chip isn't warned there's a hired gunman after him, it's bound to make the gunman's job easier.'

Sam suddenly swung his horse round and he scanned the hills. The fierce sunlight streaked across the rocks and narrow tracks, bouncing off the hillside and forming a screen that made the terrain almost invisible.

'What are you doing?' Dee cried.

'If there is someone up there, I was hoping to spot the glint of a gun.'

'You are making yourself a sitting target.' His reluctance to move tried Dee's patience. 'Let's get on. You are a proper greenhorn, Sam.'

'I've a hunch.'

'Sam, life is never easy out here in the West. Even a twenty-mile trip from Hometown to Camp Waterfall can be perilous. The climate is soul-destroying at this time of the year; there is always the danger of attacks from marauding Indians or hold-ups from gangs of outlaws. When you are out in front with a good, strong horse the sensible thing is to keep running.'

'I'm no fool, Dee! If the gunman following us is Ben Wild, I figure for a city slum boy he won't be much of a rider. He's got to get down from the hilltop if he's been trailing us.'

'What's the point in trying to trap him?'

'We'll take him prisoner.'

'It makes more sense to race ahead and warn Chip.'

The argument went on a second too long. There was a crack of a rifle from above, a sharp echo and a whining sound before a bullet swirled down the hillside and kicked up the dust inches from Sam's horse.

The near miss proved the placid and brave temperament of the Morgan breed. It fidgeted slightly and then backed off a few yards. Sam wheeled his horse and galloped in a sprint to draw abreast of Dee.

'What did I tell you?' she stormed.

'We're out of range, now.'

'Then, let's get going.'

'Not too hasty, Dee.'

'Oh! For crying out aloud!'

She urged the fast saddle-horse into a charge, covering the next quarter of a mile in a few seconds. Sam made no attempt to catch up with her, trotting his horse and continually looking over his shoulder.

Then a rumble like thunder caused him to halt his horse. Rocks tumbled from the hillside and a thick dust cloud swelled above them as they landed on the hard, dry ground. A horse appeared with a rider. Sam recognized Ben Wild. His features were screwed up in sheer panic as he lost control of the animal. Ben tried to wrestle with reins and hold a rifle at the same time. His feet fell loose from the stirrups and although the intelligent horse was carefully picking a route down the narrow tracks, his novice rider hampered him by tugging on the reins.

Loose stone caused the horse to stumble and Ben stared petrified at the long drop beneath. He pulled savagely on the reins, convinced it was the only way of stopping the horse. The animal protested with a nervous whinnying and reared up high on his front legs and, when he dropped to the ground again, the force sent his rear swinging sideways. Ben was jostled and shaken. He clung to the horse's neck, having lost his grip on the reins. The reins dropped and became entangled in the animal's stumbling gait. He fell, and tossed Ben out of the saddle. The horse rolled, four legs kicking and hit the ground at the foot of the hills. He lay there shaken, twitching, his eyes bolting in confusion and panting heavily. His rider sailed after him, his body smacking the ground face-down, sucking the breath out of him. The horse struggled to his feet, snorted, shook his head and trotted in a small circle before standing still to regain his composure.

Sam turned and rode fast to where Ben lay. The rifle was lodged between a couple of rocks some twenty yards up the hillside, but Ben was in no condition to retrieve it. Sam leaped out of the saddle, leaned over Ben and was satisfied he hadn't broken his neck. Ben groaned and moved his hands, instinctively reaching for his revolvers. Sam got to the gunman's belt first and snatched the revolvers out of the holsters. He hauled Ben to his feet. Ben swayed and rolled his eyes. His mouth bled from losing some teeth. 'Where did you get that rifle, Ben?'

'None of your business.'

'You really meant to stop us meeting up with Chip Ross.'

'Damn stupid horse let me down.'

'You should learn to ride properly.'

'Go to hell!'

'Maybe that's where you're going, Ben.'

Ben started to cringe. He was aching and sore from head to foot, and his failure in his first professional assignment made him feel sorry for himself. 'What you figuring on doing wi' me?' he asked.

'Well, I could hand you over to Sheriff Sully, but it's a long way back to Hometown. Reckon we'll take you prisoner and you can tell Chip Ross why you were paid to kill him.'

'If I were you, Sam Cotter, I shouldn't meddle in what don't concern you.'

'When a bloke fires a rifle at me I reckon that it does concern me.'

Dee rode up, glared unmercifully at Ben, and treated Sam to a generous smile. 'I guess you aren't so green, Sam.'

'Keep him covered with your little gun, Dee.'

Sam delved into his kitbag for a length of rope, bound his prisoner's hands and hoisted him in the saddle of his horse. He returned to the hillside and picked up the rifle. It was damaged beyond repair, so he stamped on it several times to break it in two.

As the trio got under way, a bunch of riders crossed the distant skyline. Sam counted nine of them and the riders were heading in the same direction as Camp Waterfall lay.

'Who are they, I wonder?' mused Dee.

'Could be a sheriff and his posse,' said Sam.

4

Progress was slow after Sam had taken Ben Wild prisoner. The young gunman was a sorry sight, still carrying the bruises Sam had inflicted on him during the stage-coach journey, and now battered from his fall off his horse and the tumble down the hillside. He seemed to be in a permanent state of fear perched on the saddle of the horse that had thrown him and Sam wasn't heartless enough to urge the small procession into a gallop, so the trio advanced upon Camp Waterfall in a gentle manner.

With frequent breaks to rest the horses they covered the twenty miles before light faded and when Chip Ross's spread came into view, Sam envied the man's lifestyle instantly. He halted his horse and took time off to study the vast expanse of flat land, ideal for exercising horses. Large corrals enclosed animals of three different breeds, the powerful and placid Morgan, the fast, sleek American Quarter Horse and the sturdy, colourful Appaloosa, leopard-spotted, favoured by the Indians.

Dee drew in beside him. 'Breathtaking, isn't it?'

While Sam couldn't take his eyes off the horses, there were herds grazing on the rich pasture that flourished by the sparkling riverside as well as the animals confined in the corrals, Dee's gaze was riveted to the magnificent waterfall that rushed over the top of a distant, rocky high ground and crashed into the river beneath. A frothy whirlpool swirled and spread till it was clawed into the river by the strong current.

'What a place to live and work,' agreed Sam.

On the south side of the river a much larger ranch than Chip's spread was dominated by a fine house and the pasture was dotted by sheep.

'That's Hoot Clackson's land,' Dee said wryly, 'and you can just see the tepees of the Crow tribe in the hills to the north.'

'You've been here before?'

'Often,' she said, and Sam frowned at her subdued tone.

But, she didn't stay in that mood for many minutes. She detected the drumming of a horse's hoofs and, peering intently beneath her enormous sun hat, her eyes took on an expression of sheer delight, and when the exciting moment was over, she fixed the oncoming rider with a gaze of sheer tenderness. Sam swallowed back his disappointment. He was conscious of how well he'd got on with Dee and was convinced he'd risen high in her esteem in the way he'd trapped the luckless Ben Wild. One glimpse of the tall, rugged and athletic Chip and Sam knew he'd never be able to compete with the successful horse-breaker.

Chip rode a huge Morgan horse at a

furious gallop and reined him to a skidding, snorting halt when he was within yards of the trio. If Dee regarded him with unstinting admiration, Sam found instant respect for the powerful, weather beaten man. He wore a buckskin suit and a wide-brimmed hat and short buckskin boots, each article brilliantly made by his friends the Crow Indians. His dark hair hung well below his neck and his sharp, brown eyes displayed the humour and contentment he enjoyed. He carried a pair of Colt revolvers and a large hunting knife in his belt. He grinned widely at his visitors, then leaned out of his beautifully embroidered saddle, more Indian handiwork, and embraced Dee in his muscular arms. He was a magnificent specimen of build and health and he swiftly brought passion into Dee's glowing features.

'I'd no idea you were coming home,' Chip said.

Hell, thought Sam. This bloke's got it all. Even his voice was deep and attractive. Chip released Dee. She would have remained speechless if Chip hadn't referred to her companions. He nodded at the bound Ben and took notice of his swollen face. 'What have you got against this kid, Dee? Didn't he appreciate your singing?'

'Ben Wild isn't a joke. He was on his way to kill you.'

Chip's friendly eyes narrowed and his square jaw dropped. Sam saw the dangerous side of his character, and realized he'd better remember it.

'When he's fit enough to talk maybe he'll tell us who hired him; if he isn't talking, maybe my friends the Crow tribe will loosen his tongue.'

Ben shivered with fright. He was cornered like a skunk. Sully would soon get rid of him because he knew too much of the crooked lawman's dealings, while he was convinced Chip Ross wouldn't waste time on him.

'We know who hired him,' said Sam.

Chip raised his eyebrows. 'Hello, sailor . . . '

'I'm not a sailor.'

'You sure dress like one.'

'I'm a horseman from England.'

'Interesting.'

Dee intervened and explained what a great help Sam had been to her since they'd met. She also informed him of the conversation she had overheard at the stage-stop.

Chip nodded solemnly, showing no surprise. 'It's no great secret that Clackson wants my land and the territory to the north where the Crow tribe has settled. He's already started to run down the livestock on his ranch and sack some of the hired hands.'

'What's his game? Is he just greedy?' asked Sam.

'He reckons the coming of the railway will kill off the need for horses and I'll be only too glad to sell out cheaply, then he'll have the Crow moved on and sell the whole of the land to the railway barons at a huge profit.'

'There will always be a need for horses!' protested Sam.

'Even if there wasn't I ain't selling. This is my home, and Clackson knows I'm as stubborn as a moke and as independent as a tomcat.'

'And that's why he wants you killed,' concluded Dee.

Chip regarded the hapless Ben Wild with a scornful look. 'Clackson will have to hire someone more professional than this poor son-of-a-gun. Let's all go and have supper.'

They unsaddled the horses and let them run free. Ben Wild was locked in a barn and a couple of Crow hired hands were entrusted with his keeping.

Sam noticed that Chip relied on the Indians to help him run the place, and despite their reputation of savage fighters, Chip had won them over, paid them proper wages and treated them as equals. His whole attitude to the so-called squatters had blackened his name in Hometown, where he was no longer welcome.

Although Chip spoke to his redskin hired hands with a cordial approach, they stared sullenly at the visitors and Chip warned Sam, that just because he was trusted by the Crow, it didn't mean they had stopped hating the white man and they continued to perform their rites and keep their traditional customs as usual. 'If a young buck had to steal your horse, Sam, as one of the rites to enrol him as a full-fledged warrior, he'll do it. Remember it!'

They had supper and Chip was generous enough to rig out Sam in cowboy's gear, that he had no more use for, and was far more suitable in this climate and country than the heavy woollens he was wearing. Sleeping quarters were arranged.

'You'll need to rest up before setting out for Hometown,' Chip said, and with his eyes set exclusively upon Dee, he added, 'but stay as long as you like.'

'I have to get back soon. My singing engagement starts this weekend.'

'You haven't grown tired of that lark then.'

'No, Chip. I love to sing . . . '

'There are other things in life.'

They were speaking sharply to each other and without regard for the presence of Sam, who wished he was somewhere else. He turned and stared out of the window. The setting sun was huge and looked as if it was turning the land into a furnace. Sam peered at the distant shadows and couldn't make up his mind what caused the shadows to dart along the wide trail leading to Chip's ranch.

The couple in the room behind him were still digging up past differences.

'You have told me a dozen times I should pack up my career and come and share your homestead, Chip.'

'And why don't you?'

'We've been through it all before.'

'You fled to New Orleans because I wanted you here.'

'I came back for no other reason than I missed you.'

'Or was it that lewd crowd at the Centre you missed?'

'Chip! That's a foul thing to say.'

'Yes, I'm sorry . . . '

'You know why I couldn't settle here. I'm just scared of the Indians that prowl around the place.'

'Chip!' cried Sam, swinging away from the window and cutting into the couple's quarrel, 'there are nine horsemen coming this way.'

Chip strode straight out of doors. These were anxious days for him because of the threat of the railway cutting across his land and he treated strangers with suspicion. As the riders pulled up in a dusty cloud outside the homestead, Chip's suspicion turned to hostility.

Rick Sully led the posse, and they were an unsavoury mob of ugly and brutal characters. In comparison, Poker Dines, the deputy, looked almost friendly.

It was obvious that Chip and Sully had clashed before and the fat, bustling sheriff held no terrors for the horse breeder. Chip told him calmly, 'I've made it plain to you before, you ain't welcome here.'

'I'm on business, Ross, and I have to cross your land to conduct it.'

Chip realized Sully's business meant interfering with the Crow tribe in the hills, and as their friend he took on the role of go-between and peacemaker. 'I take it you're heading for the Indian lodge?'

'I'm looking for Nickel Joe, the Indian trader. Has he been this way today?'

'Maybe.'

'That ain't no answer. I'm the law and if you think you can obstruct me, I reckon a spell in my jail will help you think again.'

'Nickel Joe's been with the Crow people all day. What do you want him for?'

'A tip-off. He's selling rifles and whisky to the savages. That's illegal trading.'

'Nickel Joe knows that. He's an honest and reliable man, and realizes the danger of putting rifles and whisky in the Indians' hands.'

'Well, Ross, I guess you'd better ride up there along with my boys. I need a neutral witness and you can see for yourself.'

Chip took a quick glance at the posse. Each rider was armed with the latest repeating rifle in addition to a pair of revolvers. The posse were a reckless mob of trouble makers and shooting Indians was fair game to them, but dangerous situations like this had to be averted because, however outnumbered and poorly equipped the Crow tribe were, they were too brave and proud to be ill-treated without fighting back.

Sensing trouble, Chip warned Dee to stay in the homestead and suggested that Sam looked after her, but she protested strongly, insisting she'd be safe, despite her fear of the Indians on the place. 'I think Sam should go with you, Chip,' she said.

Chip stared the young man straight in the eye. 'What about it, pardner?'

'I'm with you.'

'Steady on, lad. It ain't that simple.'

'You're my kind of man, Chip.'

'That's as maybe, but if the shooting starts, you've got to choose whose side you're on. That means defending Indians against the sheriff and his mob.'

'I'm no pal of Sully's.'

'Look, lad, I won't blame you if you back out.'

'I'm not backing out.'

'This will make you an enemy of Rick Sully and your name will be mud in Hometown. He'll probably find a reason for kicking you out of the town.'

Sam gave his reply by thrusting the pair of Colt revolvers, he'd taken off Ben Wild, in the holsters of his newly acquired leather belt. 'Shall we get the horses?'

The two men were soon astride a pair of Morgan horses. Rick Sully narrowed his mean eyes at Sam. 'I won't forget this, Cotter.'

Then he hesitated and indicated to Chip to take the lead. Chip was

76

amused, convinced the tough sheriff didn't really relish an encounter with the Crow tribe. 'Don't you know the way, Sully?'

Sully was too cunning to stick his neck out. 'The Indians be your friends. They'll not start anything if you are with us.'

'Leave them alone and there wouldn't be any need for this silly exercise.'

'Get going before it's dark.'

Chip and Sam rode in front. Leaving the river and the ranch in their wake they headed for the hills. At the foot of the hills on a square of flat land the Crow tribe had erected an avenue of conical-shaped tepees. At this moment the tepees were deserted as the warriors, their squaws, the children and the young bucks had congregated around a shabby covered wagon drawn by a single piebald horse. Trading with Nickel Joe was a leisurely business. The tall, thin nomad sold his wares from a standing position at the rear of the wagon. His customers had all the time in the world to examine the goods and bargain with the trader. Since many of the Crow menfolk earned dollars from Chip when they were employed on roundups, grooming the horses, breaking them in for riding or the long drives to horse fairs and to the army forts to sell the animals, trading with Nickel Joe was more business-like. He fixed his prices and the old-fashioned barter system was only used when Joe wanted the special curios and souvenirs fashioned by the tribe. The constant buzz that accompanied the selling and buying faded suddenly as the procession of horsemen filed along the avenue between the tepees.

Chip and Sam rode several yards ahead of the sheriff and his posse, and although the Crow warriors fanned out and formed a circle, abandoning business with the Indian trader to greet Chip, they adopted a different attitude when Rick Sully showed his face. The warriors stared in hostile fashion at their natural enemies and their hands went for their long hunting knives. Chip was fully conscious of the dangerous situation. It was an insult to the tribe for a white man to enter the lodge without being invited, although Chip enjoyed the Crow hospitality to the full.

He decided to get the charade over as quickly as possible and see Sully and his mob make a hasty retreat. 'I have escorted the sheriff of Hometown here to inspect Nickel Joe's goods. I'm sure it will take only a few minutes, then we'll leave you in peace.'

Nickel Joe swung out of his wagon and looked up at Sully. 'I'm an honest trader with nothing to hide. Why do you want to inspect my goods?'

Sully slid out of the saddle and stood among the assembly. Poker Dines followed his example and stood shoulder to shoulder with his boss. The ruffians who posed as Sully's posse held their rifles menacingly. The Indians growled in dissent and stood their ground. Chip was anxious that nobody acted recklessly. At this short range between the two enemies, hand-to-hand fighting would result in terrible carnage. Nickel Joe's common sense helped to regain the peace. He invited Sully to climb into the wagon, but when Sully declined he betrayed himself. His usual ruthless cunning deserted him, and Chip was convinced the man was nervous at being in the Crow stronghold and showed a desperation for completing his mission.

He immediately spotted the long, wooden tool-box fixed to the side of the wagon. 'You ain't bluffing me, Joe.'

'Bluffing?'

Nickel Joe shrugged his thin shoulders and blinked in puzzlement. Sully ignored him and muttered to Poker, 'Keep him covered.'

Sully kicked open the lid of the tool-box, then dived in with both hands. He straightened up, a gloating expression on his podgy features, holding a canvas canteen full of whisky and a repeater rifle. 'Honest trader, are you? Well, explain these illegal goods?'

Nickel Joe looked on helplessly. Chip was convinced he was innocent. Nobody could act as confused and bewildered as the humble trader displayed at the sight of the hidden wares. He shook from head to foot and it paved the way for the sheriff to blossom out in his most brutal fashion. Sully grabbed the poor wretch and handcuffed him. 'This is a hanging offence, and you are under arrest!'

Chip knew it was a frame-up by the way Sully had immediately searched the tool-box, but to openly accuse him now would only influence the restless Indians to charge forward and attempt to release the trader.

He remained silent. The Crow warriors looked at him for guidance, but Chip shook his head at them. They lowered their eyes and curled their lips surlily.

Sully was in his element. His posse had the mutinous Indians covered and he bounced round to glare at the warriors. 'A box full of rifles and firewater, eh! That's a bad mixture for you savages to get hold of. You know you ain't allowed either and I ought to clap the lot of you in jail.'

The warriors fidgeted uneasily. To their nomadic and free nature, imprisonment was the worst punishment they could endure. Sully leered at them, convinced he held the upper hand, and announced curtly, 'You can go free, but make sure you have quit this stretch of land by dawn tomorrow. If you don't a hundred soldiers will come.'

He ordered Nickel Joe into his wagon and the procession moved out of the Crows' lodge. The warriors watched in silence. When the procession was within sight of the river, Chip rode up abreast of Sully. 'You filthy buzzard, that was a scheme to get rid of the Crow tribe, and I don't have to even think who set it up.'

'Are you saying I'm a crooked sheriff?'

'Saying it and meaning it.'

Sully laughed in Chip's face. 'Come to Nickel Joe's hanging in a couple of days' time.'

5

Chip and Sam rode on ahead of Sully and his posse and reached Chip's homestead well in advance of the arrested Nickel Joe and his escort. Chip swung out of his saddle and bounded across the yard between the ranch-house and the outbuildings and burst into the barn. He emerged driving a scowling, uneasy Ben Wild in front of him and Chip's mood was as dark as the gloom that gathered across the fertile plains.

Sam dismounted and together with Chip they stood guard over their prisoner. Sully and his posse crossed the river and rode on to Chip's land, heading for Clackson's spread where they intended to camp for the night and satisfy themselves of the Crow tribe's dawn departure.

Chip confronted Sully, holding up his

hand as a signal to stop. Sully leaned out of his saddle and his features were disgruntled as he recognized the brash, young gunman held by Sam. 'What's the game, Ross?' he demanded.

'You've arrested an innocent man and I ain't going to let you get away with it.'

'You saw the guns and whisky?'

'Aye, maybe I did, but I'll bet fifty of my best horses they were put in Nickel Joe's wagon by your men when it was parked for the night.'

'That'll take some proving.'

'You knew exactly where to look for the illegal goods, Sully. That might stand up as evidence in a court of law.'

Sully laughed vulgarly as if Chip had made a lewd remark. 'Sure, you bring a case against me and we'll have Hoot Clackson, the town's magistrate listen to it.'

Chip was jolted by Sully's retort. He'd been out of touch with Hometown for so long he hadn't considered Clackson being elected a magistrate.

Between them, a crooked sheriff and an evil magistrate, they had the town pretty well at their mercy. Chip recovered quickly and challenged Sully with his original idea. 'What about a deal?'

Sully was too greedy a man not to listen. He squinted down at Chip. 'What's the deal?'

'I'll hand over this kid, who Clackson paid fifty dollars to kill me, in exchange for Nickel Joe.'

'What a load of moonshine, Ross!'

'If there's no deal, I'm riding into Independence with Ben Wild, and he's going to confess to the county marshal. It's up to you.'

Sully was forced to take Chip's offer seriously. The mere mention of the county marshal was something that had to be heeded. Neither Clackson nor the sheriff would welcome a senior lawman enquiring into the affairs that were taking place in the small town. But, standing beside Sam, it was Ben Wild suffering an attack of the shivers who knew he had most to lose. He stared bleakly at his captor. Ben was a pitiful sight, bruised and downcast; he had quickly concluded that his journey from the slums of Chicago to the West to satisfy an ambition to be a professional gunman was the dream of a foolish man. There was a weak, patronizing smile on his pale face as he pleaded with Sam. 'Don't hand me over to Sully. I won't stand a chance. He'll have to shoot me to stop me talking.'

'What chance were you going to give Chip Ross, eh?'

'Look, let me stay. I'll throw in my lot with you. We can be pals?'

'You ain't in any position to make deals, Ben. And, speaking for myself, I couldn't trust you any further than I could throw you.'

Sam ignored Ben, who was in such a state of fear he was prepared to do anything to stay out of Sully's hands. The sheriff was deep in thought following Chip's suggestion. At the outset it had seemed a simple plan to move the Crow tribe and although it meant sacrificing an innocent man's life, that wouldn't weigh heavily on Sully's conscience.

'Can't you make up your mind?' Chip taunted him.

'Clever buzzard, ain't you?'

'Smart enough to tell this is all a put-up job.'

'You are so damn sure I can't risk having the county marshal nosing around my patch.'

'Pretty sure, Sully.'

'I've got nine gunmen here. What chance . . . '

Sully never ended his threat. Chip drew his pair of Colt revolvers with a speed and smoothness that was quite awesome. A split second before he was standing relaxed, looking questioningly up at Sully, and now the sheriff was sucking nervously for moisture to ease his dry mouth as the pair of Colt revolvers were aimed straight at him. Sully heard the movement of his men as they reached for their guns, but he had no desire to fall if a shoot-out began. 'Hold it, boys. Let's keep this peaceful.'

He stared at Chip, torn between admiration and hatred for the man's gunslinging ability. 'What do I gain from this deal, Ross?'

'You'll save Clackson from a lot of embarrassment if I hand Ben Wild over to you.'

'If I can't pin nothing on Nickel Joe and there ain't been no illegal trading with the Crow tribe then I ain't got no reason to move them off this territory.'

'That's summed it up pretty well, Sully.'

The sheriff turned in his saddle and ordered Nickel Joe to be released. The Indian trader brought the wagon round in a full circle and positioned it close to Chip and Sam, and the exchange was completed when Ben Wild was pushed forward, screaming hysterically and hurling vile language in all directions. The young gunman was hoisted up behind Poker Dines, who rode the biggest horse, and the posse retreated sulkily.

Nickel Joe sat in his wagon, so confused and dazed that he failed to utter a word of thanks to his rescuer. He simply grinned hugely with enormous relief and then muttered a prayer to the darkening skies above. Chip invited him to stay the night, but the trader felt he would be more at home with the Crow people. 'Tell them they do not have to quit their homes,' Chip called out to him as he set off.

'I tell them what a good friend they have,' replied Nickel Joe.

Chip peered in the direction of Clackson's sheep farm and watched the shadows of the posse flitting along the wide track.

'You settled Sully's hash good and proper,' said Sam.

'Don't be so enthusiastic. This battle is far from over and I'm the under-dog. Clackson will try anything to get me off my spread and Sully is looking forward to the day when he can throw me inside his jail and lose the key.'

'I guess I'm not too popular with the bloke, either.'

'Do you have to go back to Hometown? I can find you a job here.'

'Thanks, Chip, but I have to take Dee back and I'd like a crack at that Pony Express.'

The mention of Dee caused Chip to look surprised. 'We've left her alone too long.'

They put the horses away and strolled into the house. It was cool after the sultry evening but oddly silent and, after a tour of the rooms, calling out Dee's name as they went, they were forced to conclude she wasn't at home. Chip hurried to the quarters where the Indian boys had already taken to their bunks and shook them into wakefulness. 'Where has my woman gone?'

The two young bucks who shared the duties of house-boys between them, regarded Chip lazily and thought it strange he appeared so distressed.

'White woman gone to waterfall to

see the whirlpool by moonlight.'

'Damn your hides! Why didn't you take care of her?'

He stormed out and glanced solemnly at Sam, framed in the doorway of the room. 'We ain't finished for the night. Dee's along by the river and Sully and his outlaws ain't far away. That makes me feel uncomfortable.'

Sleeping out of doors, despite the fine night, wasn't for Sully and his mob. Their horses were put away in a small corral and the nine riders strolled arrogantly into the long bunkhouse. Despite the objections of the three shepherds who lived there, Sully took over the place, selecting the best bunks and by using his authority ordered the shepherds to rustle up some food for their visitors. When they had withdrawn to the cookhouse, Sully called his men around him. He loved the role of commander and after drawing up a rota for outside guard duties, reminding the men the savage redskins were not many acres away, his attention was diverted to the problem of what to do about Ben Wild.

The young gunman sat on the edge of his bunk, thoroughly miserable and staring at the dirt floor. Matters had got worse for him by the minute. Chip Ross didn't have to exchange him for the Indian trader, and Sam Cotter did nothing to dissuade him. One day he'd get both of them!

'See here, kid,' said Sully, 'I reckon the safest thing for me to do, would be to tell Poker to take you outside and shoot you. Then I know you wouldn't ever open your mouth to strangers again.'

'I won't talk out of turn. Hoot Clackson's hiring of me to kill Ross won't go any further, I promise.'

'But, you ain't done the job, have you?'

'The stupid horse bucked when I fired . . . '

'And, now you haven't got any guns. What kinda hired gunman are you without a gun?'

Ben hadn't an answer to Sully's criticism. Sam Cotter had licked him twice in close combat but he couldn't admit that to the tough sheriff.

The food arrived, steaming pans of beans with pots of coffee. Sully rubbed his hands together greedily. 'Good-o! That smells great!'

He waddled up to the long table in the centre of the bunkhouse, dropped his fat behind into a chair and attacked the food. Ben frowned, wondering what his fate was going to be, yet, Sully had suddenly lost interest in him. Then, with a mouth crammed with beans, Sully turned in his chair. 'Seven days I'll give you to kill Chip Ross. You'll stay behind when we leave at sun-up. I'll give you a pair of revolvers, but you won't need a horse. Oh, and if the job ain't done in a week, I'll be sending someone to do it for me, and he'll put you under, too.'

★   ★   ★

The idea of Dee roaming along the river bank at night, despite the fine moon, haunted both Chip and Sam, and by the time they left the house they had broken into a sprint. There was not a minute to spare in which to saddle the horses so they ran all the way to where the waterfall cascaded into the river. Chip had built a solid, timber bridge that spanned the river at the deepest end and it was a pleasant spot to stand and watch the whirlpool spin especially when the golden moonlight was caught up in its web.

Crude laughter echoed towards them and when the laughter was mingled with a petrified scream, Chip drew his revolvers. Sam did the same. There was nobody on the bridge, but peering across the river on to Clackson's land, they saw Dee struggling between two of Sully's burly outlaws. It was hard to tell at that distance if Sully's guards had snatched the young woman from the bridge and dragged her on to their side of the river to amuse themselves in an act of vile rape, or kidnapping was their aim. Chip led the charge across the bridge with Sam at his heels. The cruel, mocking laughter continued, but for some reason Dee's screaming had stopped.

Chip decided against a gunfight. With Dee in the middle of the affray the result would be disastrous, but the two ruffians' hands were fully engaged mauling Dee to draw their own guns. One thug was stifling Dee's screams for help by gripping her throat and pressing on her soft flesh with his two powerful thumbs. His mate was ripping the cotton shirt from her body, the sight of which infuriated Chip. He bellowed the scream of a madman and charged into the fray with no thought of fighting like a gentleman. He threw punches and kicked out impulsively, taking on the two thugs at once, but when Sam singled out his opponent, an overweight piece of flab, and coolly hit him with measured, two-fisted punches, it relieved Chip of being outnumbered.

Sam boxed with the skill taught to him by an old bare-fisted, prize-fighter who had kept the local tavern in the Sussex village where Sam had worked. His tall and slender build allowed him to dance round his opponent and the blows snaked out plastering the ugly oaf's face, splitting his lips, drawing bad teeth and closing his bloodshot eyes. The ruffian spat and swore. He gasped breathlessly and, when his bandy legs gave way beneath him, Sam finished him off with a vicious uppercut that landed him in a heap close to the water's edge. Sam turned to assist Chip, but the horse-breeder, experienced in rough-houses at horse fairs where tempers ran riot, had made short work of the villain molesting Dee, and was now bending over her. He looked up at Sam, anxious and alarmed. 'She can't speak. That skunk almost bored holes in her throat.'

Chip worked on the semi-unconscious woman and her breathing grew more even, but when she tried to talk the result was like the growl of a frightened dog. She could only reply to Chip's questions by either nodding or shaking her head. It was ten minutes before she was able to stand up. The thugs on the ground were recovering. Sam kept his eyes riveted to them. 'What we going to do with these blokes, Chip?'

'Toss 'em in the river. Cool down their ardour.'

'What if they can't swim?'

'Who cares?' said Chip, glancing sadly at Dee.

Sam grinned at Chip, thinking he wasn't serious, but he meant what he said and hurled each of the thugs in turn into the fast-flowing river. Then between them, Chip and Sam carried Dee back to the house. They both felt awkward putting her to bed in her room and Chip could have sent one of his houseboys to the Crow lodge and enlisted the help of a young squaw to nurse Dee, or even better employ the services of the talented, young beauty Gentle Sunrise, who did wonders for her people with medicinal herbs and nature cures. Gentle Sunrise would have come willingly, but Dee would not tolerate an Indian touching her.

'It isn't empty prejudice,' said Chip, persuading Dee to take tiny sips of cold water from a mug. 'Like so many kids out here during the past decade her folks were slaughtered by the Sioux tribe.'

Dee widened her eyes at Chip and shook her head in a strong protest. She wasn't able to speak, but she was fully aware of what Chip was telling Sam, and now she protested against having an Indian treat her, however clever and dedicated Gentle Sunrise was reputed to be. She made signs to Chip that she wanted pen and paper to write down instructions. She scrawled in huge letters and handed the notepaper to Chip. He read it quickly. 'Will you ride back to Hometown in the morning, Sam?'

'Something I can do?'

'Sure thing. Dee's worried about letting down the audience at the Centre but she won't be singing for a while yet. Hoot Clackson runs things there and you'll have to break the news to him. She also needs a doctor. Turner is the best man, but he stays put in town on account he won't ride since being thrown a coupla years back. Use my buggy and bring him out here.'

Sam's plans to return to Hometown to apply for a riding job with Pony Express were being thwarted, but he couldn't refuse taking on this mission of mercy for Dee's sake.

It was barely light when he harnessed his horse between the shafts of the buggy, and the trip had taken on a sense of urgency since Dee was running a high fever, a shock reaction from the assault she suffered last night.

Sam urged the horse into a fast trot, hoping to cover as many miles as the cool morning would allow. The strong horse responded heartily and progress was swift, but as the sun broke free from the thin cloud covering the plains, Sam observed the string of horses crossing open country, the riders languid in their saddles. Sully was easily recognizable by his sagging frame and it was obvious the sheriff had got his posse on the move even before Sam had set out. They had the advantage over him of not keeping to the main trail between Camp Waterfall and Hometown, but were using the tracks carved out by herds of cattle on minor trails.

Sam counted the number of riders, curious to learn if the two thugs Chip had tossed into the river last night had survived. The posse including Sully and Poker Dines was still nine-strong, but Sam wondered how the two guards had explained their wet clothing and cut faces to Sully. If the thugs had escaped drowning what fate had befallen the luckless Ben Wild? He wasn't included in the party heading for Hometown and it needed little imagination on Sam's part to consider Sully had ordered the young gunman to be shot in cold blood for failing to kill Chip, and worse still, to fall into his enemy's hands and to be used as a hostage that wrecked Sully's plans to remove the Crow tribe from north of the river. Sam felt some sympathy for the brash, but misguided youth from the slums of Chicago, who was less at home in the West than Sam was himself. Ben's inability to handle a horse under difficult conditions had led to his capture and even if his gun-play was impressive, Sam had the edge over him because he was an expert horse-man. It was a question of what was the most vital of a man in the wild frontier, a horse or his guns?

The posse vanished from sight beneath the shimmering heat and Sam was content to plod along, knowing full well the horse and buggy wouldn't cover the twenty gruelling miles to Hometown in a day although a single rider on a powerful horse could. He travelled in the shadows of the hills, a notorious hunting ground for bandits and outlaws, where narrow canyons proved to be dangerous traps to the innocent rider. The sparkling river, that divided Camp Waterfall into three territories drifted on his right, and when he sighted a pleasant spot, sheltered by a clump of willow trees, on the river bank, he decided to camp for the night.

He released the weary horse from the shafts of the buggy and tethered him to a tree, but with enough freedom to drink from the river and feed off the lush pasture. Sam built a fire, cooked beans in a pan and brewed coffee in a pot. He studied the stars for a while and then laid out his bedding-roll in the buggy where there was more shelter from the lively breeze that whipped off the river. He reckoned he was sleeping in the loneliest spot on earth. There was hardly a sound. The willow trees rustled but only discreetly as if to create any annoying sound would be inhospitable, while the river sneaked past in a gentle flow.

Sam slept heavily. It had been an adventurous, tiring twenty-four hours since he'd set out from Hometown, escorting Dee, to warn Chip a gunman had been hired to shoot him. Since he'd met Chip he liked and respected the horse-breeder and there hadn't been a dull moment, which reduced his eagerness to join the Pony Express outfit.

The sudden whinnying of his horse brought him to with a start. The scampering of fast footsteps in the frail light of a new dawn caused him to sweep the blanket aside and vault over the side of the buggy. His horse reared as a lithe, half-naked Indian buck ripped the rope from the tree. Sam drew one pistol and aimed it at the thief. The light was poor and Sam realized he wasn't the expert marksman to hit the thief at long range, and he feared he might shoot the horse by accident. He tried to bluff the Indian by shouting a warning. 'Hold it! I'll shoot you down like a dog.'

The Indian buck turned and showed Sam his bronzed face. He grinned widely. His teeth were small and polished white. His big brown eyes were full of mischief and his slender frame was as athletic as any young man could wish it to be. His behaviour puzzled Sam. The young buck acted almost friendly to the pale-face, when by tradition they were sworn enemies. He captured the horse and leaped on the animal's bare back, then with a triumphant wave to the stranded Sam, he rode hard towards the open plains.

Sam sank to the ground, bitter with himself. He'd been trusted to undertake an urgent errand and had failed miserably. What good was a buggy without a horse when he was still ten miles from Hometown?

6

Sam sat on the river bank, a brooding expression in his eyes, at a complete loss as to what to do next. The sun blazed down on to the water, feeding it with golden nuggets. The dry plains went on as far as the grey hills on the skyline. He was left with a buggy, a horse's harness and saddle, and a length of rope. He cursed that handsome, Indian buck for leaving him in such a dilemma. The horse didn't even belong to Sam. It had been hired from Anvil Smith, who owned Hometown's livery, a peaceful giant of a man, but then Sam had only seen the man in a good mood.

He'd discarded the notion of walking the ten miles into town. His mission was to collect Doc Turner, who never rode a horse, and bring him back to Camp Waterfall. 'Oh, what wouldn't I give for a horse!' Sam muttered.

His only hope of help would be from travellers using the main trail between Camp Waterfall and Hometown. Perhaps someone would have a horse to sell, but Sam was flat broke. Maybe he could barter his guns for a horse. He was convinced a horse was more valuable than a pair of revolvers, yet, it was more prudent to own both.

By noon, the sun overhead was torrid, and he hadn't seen a soul. He'd moved to the shelter of the willow trees and the cooler climate tempted him to doze, but the memory of a thief at large kept him awake. Then, a sound, rumbling like thunder from one of the canyons in the foothills beyond caused him to swing round and try to locate the reason for the canyons to become alive, sending echoes across the isolated land.

The rumblings were followed by a huge dust cloud, sweeping towards him. Sam had not been in the country long enough to understand the strange phenomenon of a sandstorm rising out of a still, hot day. He pulled his neckerchief up over his nose as a precaution against breathing in the thick dust. The yellow cloud rolled towards him and he was about to flatten himself on to the ground when a chorus of whinnying pierced the cloud. Sam sat motionless, too stunned to take in the sound that was normally so common to him. The cloud rolled past him and the breeze from the river thinned it. The thunderous sound increased to a deafening roar and Sam glimpsed the long, swishing tails and thick, hairy coats of a herd of wild mustang. Sam counted forty bucking heads and reasoned this wasn't a mirage that appeared before him. The herd was real, having rested in the canyon till it was time to move down to the river to drink. The cloud of dust dispersed in the herd's wake as the wild horses charged into the river. They drank and swam, unaware of being watched by a stranger, desperately in need of a horse.

Sam gathered up his length of rope, formed a generous loop and secured it with a slip-knot. He went stealthily forward to the water's edge. The horses were swimming with their backs to him, heads well clear of the river's surface. The mustangs were a motley collection. Some were small and shaggy, their growth stunted, others, of medium height were better bred and looked strong and healthy, while outstanding among the herd were two powerful stallions, one pure black and another dark grey. As splendid as the pair of stallions looked, Sam disregarded them. He had to think in terms of selecting an animal, capturing it, then breaking him in for harnessing between the shafts of the buggy. It all had to be done in the shortest possible time and he knew he couldn't succeed with two wild and angry leaders of the herd.

He cast his eyes upon a sturdy chestnut-coloured animal, that reminded him of a Welsh Cob. The strong, little horse swam boldly and apart from the rest of the herd. He suggested to Sam an independent nature, but more important, there was room to throw the rope and trap it by the neck.

But, Sam knew he would only get one chance. If the rope fell short or wide, it would alarm the whole herd and it would stampede back on to dry land and home to the protective custody of the hills. He had roped horses in fields back in Sussex with a skill that was quite awesome to the other stable lads, but he was out of regular practice, following his emigration to this new country.

The chestnut mustang suddenly took it into his head to turn and swim down river. He gave Sam a better target and Sam took the chance immediately. He swung the rope above his head six times, working up a speed till it whirred. Then he sent the loop-end of the rope sailing above the river. The rope hovered, then dropped. Sam watched, holding his breath. It was a good shot, but not as accurate as he wanted. Three-quarters of the loop rested on the horse's head. It startled him into a nervous bellowing. He shook his head and the loop slipped further down, taking in both ears and his mouth. Another frantic shaking of the head and Sam's luck held. The loop cupped the horse's chin. He was captured. His bellowing was taken up by the rest of the herd. Fear, anger and wildness registered in the horses' stark eyes and ears, stiff and upright. They swung their heads to see what the danger was and saw the stranger with the rope. Fearing a similar fate, the stallions let out a duet of whinnying that echoed along the river, giving ample warning to the herd. The horses immediately abandoned the river and galloped to the shore, sending silver waves against the river bank, and then following the stallions they charged across the flat land, heading for the foothills and bustled their way into the narrow passage of the canyon. After they had vanished from sight, the horse now in Sam's possession went frantic, now that he'd been segregated from the herd. He bucked and reared and Sam realized he had a fight on his hands to bring the angry, frightened animal ashore. The tough, little horse, which Sam compared to a Welsh Cob, quickly earned himself the name of 'Taffy' and although Sam spoke to him gently, Taffy dug his hoofs into the muddy, river-bed and anchored himself.

Sam's stamina began to let him down and he felt himself being dragged into the river. He had enough rope to play with to secure it to the trunk of the stoutest willow tree and tying it firmly, Sam took a breather while watching Taffy fighting against odds. 'You won't shift that tree, Taffy, old son. Why not come out of the water?'

Taffy eyed his captor with a hostile expression and tugged on the rope relentlessly. The slip-knot tightened and threatened to choke him. Taffy panicked, reared and rolled off-balance into the river, kicking violently.

Sam played out more rope from the tree and dashed into the river. He slackened the loop round Taffy's neck. Taffy shook his head, coughed once, and with Sam's help struggled to his feet. The horse seemed to have gained the impression that Sam was his saviour, and when Sam spoke quietly to him, calming him down, stroking his neck and ears as he did so, Taffy playfully nudged Sam in the shoulder. Five minutes later they were friends and Sam led the horse ashore.

It was too early to trust the horse completely and Sam kept him tethered to the willow tree with enough freedom to graze the lush pasture. Sam remembered he'd brought a small bag of oats with him for the horse fodder when he'd set out the day before. He doubted if Taffy had ever tasted the succulent oats and taking the bag to the horse, he tempted him with a feed. Taffy sniffed the oats suspiciously, then munched the grain from Sam's hand and finally grew excited at the new taste, whinnying his approval by licking Sam's hand.

After the horse was well fed, Sam spent the next two hours breaking him in. Taffy didn't take kindly to the saddle and Sam let him take his fury out on the burden while still tethered to the tree. Leaves and twigs were scattered like rain and it was a cruel way to discipline the horse under a blazing sun, but Sam was short of time. He mounted the horse and for a short, exhilarating period he shared a private rodeo show with Taffy, but the bucking and twisting took too much out of the horse and he allowed Sam to ride him at a walking pace along the river bank.

Taffy now accepted Sam as his master, although there was enough spirit left in the horse not to be servile. The harnessing and backing Taffy between the shafts of the buggy was a frustrating exercise, bewildering the horse and causing Sam to lose his patience, but further bribery with a handful of oats seemed to convince

Taffy what was required of him.

They set off at a gentle pace without any badgering from Sam and as the late afternoon cooled, Taffy began to enjoy the task. It wasn't so exhausting as chasing after the two stallions at the head of the herd and pulling the buggy at his own speed suited his independence. Life in the wilds, cantering across rocky hills, uneven tracks and bumpy trails had taught him to be sure-footed, and when the sun began to dip behind the skyline, Taffy showed his appreciation of the cool climate by breaking into a gallop.

They covered the last few miles into Hometown at a breathless speed, but a fresh problem presented itself. Taffy had never experienced hordes of people, noise and the bustle of wagons, and today was worse for him as the main street was congested with a long, slow procession of army cavalry. The troopers rode in double-file, equipped for a full-scale field operation. Army mules hauled wagons crammed with supplies and at the rear four field guns were towed. At the head of the procession rode a tall, rugged officer with long, dark hair and penetrating brown eyes. He turned to glower at Sam in his buggy and his features jolted Sam as if the young man had suddenly frozen in his seat. The officer was blunt and capable and looked proud in his double-blue and gold uniform. 'Keep out of the way, lad,' he snapped in a deep voice, as Sam tried to work his horse and buggy past the column.

Sam had wanted to get in front of the column because Taffy was being hemmed in and he didn't like it. The horse's nervousness was betrayed in his unsteady gait and fierce swishing of his tail. Sam grew red with indignation. Trust the army to think they could take over anywhere they chose to enter, and this particular officer seemed as if he held mere civilians in contempt.

'My horse isn't used to crowds, mister. Will you let me pass?'

'Nobody overtakes the United States

Cavalry. And, never call an army major mister.'

Sam didn't want to cause havoc so he pulled Taffy on to the cobbled front of a row of stores and business premises. A crowd of townsfolk had collected to watch the cavalry go past. Sam gave the major a scornful glare and the expression was met by the officer and sharply returned. It was as if they had clashed before and the memory of an unpleasant contact still lingered. Sam's grimy face was lined with curiosity at the sight of the major's familiar features and he stared after the well-built, weather beaten man long after the column had reached the distant end of the main street, then veered to the right to occupy a fifteen-acre field where they intended to set up camp.

A hearty, fruity voice distracted Sam. 'There'll be trouble in town tonight. Troops and cowboys never did mix.'

Anvil Smith's huge frame and muscular arms worked feverishly over his furnace at the open front of his livery and blacksmith's shop. He spoke to nobody in particular, but his voice attracted Sam, who didn't realize he'd parked the buggy barely ten yards away from Anvil's premises. Sam had guilty thoughts about the fine horse he'd hired from Anvil and now the main street was clear of troops and Sam had to find Doc Turner and Hoot Clackson, he gently flicked the reins for Taffy to creep away. Sam was caught in the act by Anvil, who in the process of wiping the dark sweat from his face, seemed to focus his sight clearly and recognized the young stranger, Dee's friend and escort. 'Hold it there!' roared Anvil, his eyes blazing.

His sudden shout caused Taffy to rear and Sam was forced to use all his skill to prevent a runaway. He tightened the reins and Taffy came down to stand on all fours, snorting angrily and shaking his head. Anvil strode forward, gripping a red-hot poker.

'For crying out aloud, Anvil! Put that

poker down. You're scaring the day-lights out of my horse.'

As Anvil advanced, Sam could feel Taffy, tense and nervous, ready to buck and rear again.

'I'd like to know what's happened to that fine Morgan horse I hired out to you, and maybe a red-hot poker burning up your flesh will persuade you to tell me the truth.'

Sam's assessment of Anvil was proved accurate in that moment. He was hail-fellow-well-met, a town character with his enormous size and strength and joviality, but only when his mood was right. Upset the man and he could be as evil as any villain. Sam hesitated. He was too embarrassed to reply, but Anvil was impatient, and Sam could feel the fierce glow of the poker make his eyes smart. 'Your horse was stolen.'

Anvil retained his grip on the poker. Sam hoped he wouldn't press for details. Horse-thieves were as common as the stars at night, but to lose a

Morgan was something that needed explaining.

'How did it happen?'

'I camped for the night, halfway between Camp Waterfall and here, tethered the Morgan, but at the first sign of daybreak this young Crow buck rode off with him.'

Anvil narrowed his fiery eyes at Sam. His huge chest heaved and then with a vulgar curse he hurled the poker into the furnace. Sparks flew, matching his temper. 'My God! My saintly Ma and Pa. I ask for the truth and I get told this.'

'Anvil! Believe me, it's the truth.'

'I know it is, that's what makes it worse. A skinny, dumb savage steals a white man's horse. What's the matter with you, do you live in a dream?'

'This Crow buck wasn't skinny. He was fit and athletic.'

'Whatever he was he made you look a fool.'

'I never saw a living soul since I started out from Camp Waterfall, then this horse thief appears as if he came in with the dawn.'

Anvil shook his head solemnly at Sam. 'You must always be prepared for the unexpected out here. Ain't no good you wanting to be a Pony Express rider, the trail is full of hazards . . . anyway, the firm has taken on all the young men they need.'

Sam set his features hard to disguise his disappointment. He shrugged and said, 'Doesn't matter, Chip Ross has offered me work.'

Anvil pointed at the buggy. 'That belongs to him. How come you be driving it?'

Sam told him about Dee's rough treatment at the hands of Sully's men. 'She's lost her voice and is running a high fever. She needs a doctor.' Anvil squinted down at Sam and his rough manner mellowed. 'You made the journey alone, so where did you pick up that mustang?'

'I captured him from a wild herd.'

'And you broke him in to pull the buggy!'

'It took a couple of hours of hard work.'

Anvil's thick, lower lip dropped into a sulky pout. 'Only two hours, eh? You taking the rise out of me?'

'No, he's an intelligent and independent horse. I've handled scores like him in my time.'

Anvil scratched his beard. 'Reckon I figured you wrong, boy, but I can't afford to lose a Morgan horse. Just you find that horse thief and get me back my Morgan and you'll earn my respect.'

'I'll do my best . . . can I bed down with my horse in your stables tonight?'

'Still broke, eh?'

'Yes, Anvil.'

'Well, if there are horse thieves about, maybe I can do with someone to stand guard. Sure, that's a deal.'

Sam left his horse and buggy in Anvil's care and was glad to stretch his legs after the long journey driving into Hometown. It was late in the day and stores on both sides of the main street were seeing to the last of their customers' needs before putting up shutters. He found Doc Turner's surgery. It was crowded with ailing children with their anxious mothers. A flu epidemic had hit the town and by the time Sam was able to see the doctor he knew his chances of dragging the elderly physician out of town to visit one patient were slim. Doc Turner was tired and irritable. He'd got his own round to do from one end of the town to the other, calling to treat patients who were too sick to leave their beds. Sam's request struck the doctor as funny. 'You have seen what things are like here? Every doctor in town is worn out with work, and you want me to travel twenty miles to see a single patient? I'm sorry Dee Miller has lost her voice, that's bad for a singer, but I've no medicine to give you that'll do her any good. Just tell her to stop talking till her voice returns.'

The doctor showed Sam the door, despite the young man's pleading. 'I have a horse and buggy ready to leave at first light. I'll take you to Camp Waterfall and bring you back . . . '

'Son, I haven't the time.'

Sam found himself on the sidewalk staring at the closed door. Around him lamps were being lit on the premises that came alive when darkness fell. Saloons and gambling dens, and the most popular palace of entertainment, the Centre, was filling up. Off-duty soldiers in gangs headed for the bars, shoving their way past the regular cowboy customers. Sam went in. Poker Dines sat at a table near the entrance and confiscated the guns carried by the customers. He gave Sam a suspicious glance, his thin features showing the strain of the fast ride home from Camp Waterfall. His drooping eyes were bloodshot and he was unshaven. He shared the humiliation of defeat at the hands of Chip Ross as much as Sheriff Sully did, and it irked him to see someone who'd partnered Ross during the recent conflict over Nickel Joe's arrest. 'You get around, don't you, Cotter?'

'Here on business with Hoot Clackson.'

Poker Dines pulled a menacing expression from his weary eyes. 'I don't trust you. Reckon you can make trouble. What you got to see Clackson about?'

'That's between him and me.'

'Is it now? Well, I'm telling you to get out of town.'

'I'm going, as soon as dawn breaks in the morning.'

Poker had no more to say to that, but as soon as Sam mounted the stairs the deputy sent one of his cronies to warn Sully that Cotter was back in town to see Hoot Clackson. It must have spelt trouble because Sully arrived hot-foot to the Centre.

Sam was invited into Clackson's private rooms. The landowner was in a foul mood, drinking heavily and an ashtray on the small table was already filled with cigar butts. 'You got something important to say to me, then say it and be on your way, boy!'

'Dee can't sing for you. She's lost her voice.'

Clackson slammed the glass he held down on the table. The glass shattered and amber liquid splashed on to the floor. 'What! Damn you, boy. There's a hundred troops in town and Dee will fill the place at each performance. How the hell did she lose her voice?'

Sam frowned at him innocently. 'You haven't heard?'

'How would I!'

'I figured Sully might have told you?'

'What's it got to do with Sully?'

'Two of his thugs tried to rape her. They half strangled her before Chip Ross rescued her.'

'And this happened at Camp Waterfall?' stormed Clackson, his eyes full of fury.

'I think you know what Sully and his mob were doing there,' Sam told him calmly and turned towards the door. Clackson cleared the small table of bottles with a wild sweep of his hand and, in his drunken rage, he declared,

'Sully does nothing right. The Crow tribe are still squatting on land the railway wants, and now he's deprived me of hundreds of dollars by crippling my star singer.'

Sam waited to hear no more. He'd delivered his message and now he was going to snatch a few hours' sleep before heading out to Camp Waterfall.

He strolled through the saloon below and sidestepped a scuffle that was in process between an army trooper and a burly cowboy. Over went a table, spilling cards, drinks and coins on to the floor. The next instant it was a free-for-all with a score of soldiers taking on the rest of the customers. Sam struggled to get out of the place. It was almost impossible while dodging flying bottles and avoiding becoming involved in the fight. Then at the height of the battle, the swing doors were pushed open and in strode the major, who commanded the cavalry detachment, closely followed by two hefty sergeants.

The immaculately dressed major surveyed the scene for a moment, his features set cold and bitter, and then he shouldered his way into the mêlée, displaying his enormous strength by separating fighters by hauling them apart by the scruffs of their necks. 'Fall in outside 'A' troop. At the double!'

His order was instantly obeyed as he stood among the wreckage, taking note of the uniformed combatants, his keen eyes scanning the bloodstained sea of faces. He caught Sam looking at him in admiration for his authority and strength. 'You again? Am I such a handsome guy you can't take your eyes off me?'

Sam shook his head and muttered in confusion, 'You just remind me of someone I know, sir.'

'Well, I've never seen you before, so scat! I've work here to do.'

Sam escaped from the saloon. In his wake he heard the major shouting at his men. 'Got energy to spare have you? Well, there'll be an extra drill soon after reveille in the morning.'

Hoot Clackson stumbled down the stairs to see what all the commotion was about and was in time to corner the major as he paraded his troublesome men outside. 'I trust the Army will pay for the damage,' he scowled.

'Not all of it,' retorted the major, stiffly.

'Your men were sent here to fight Indians, not cause trouble with the locals.'

'My men are all keyed up to fight. Just give the word. It's all the hanging about that makes them bored.'

Clackson fidgeted with discomfort. He was against obstacles that had to be cleared before he was able to ask the major to clear Camp Waterfall of the Crow tribe. Chip Ross had to be moved off his land, too, and there was only one drastic way to do that. 'The railway surveyors are arriving in a week's time, so the land will have to be free by then.'

'Strikes me this is a typical example of civilian disorder,' said the major huffily, and stamped out of the saloon to march his men back to the fifteen acres of waste ground where they were living under canvas.

Sully and Poker Dines watched the brief encounter between the crimson-faced Clackson and the tall, cool army major with suspicion. The pair resented the cavalry being called in, taking it personally because they had failed to shift the Indians from their lodge. Clackson swung round and almost toppled over, regaining his balance only by clutching the table where the sheriff and his deputy sat. Their eyes met and Sully's cruel expression seemed to trigger off something of importance that raged in Clackson's mind. He collapsed into a chair and the excess of liquor gave him more courage than he normally displayed. His words were slurred, but the message was plain. 'Sully, what you going to do about those ruffians of yours who attacked Dee Miller?'

'Oh, it was just a bit of fun the boys were having.'

'Fun! The girl can't speak, let alone sing.'

'An accident,' suggested Sully, absently shuffling a pack of cards.

'Attempted rape isn't an accident. You're getting too fat and lazy; this job is too easy for you. Where were you when this brawl took place in my saloon? Feet up in your office I suppose. Well, you can shift yourself and earn your wages. Go and fetch them two outlaws of yours in, throw them in jail and we'll put them up for trial.'

'I'll see to it in the morning.'

'You ride out, now!'

'Hell, it's night-time.'

'You know where to find their hide-out. Get going, or hand me your star.'

Sully aimed the powerful man a mutinous stare, but he realized Clackson was in a position to make good his threats. The sheriff jumped to his feet and kicked the chair out of his way. His bloated face looked as sour as a bloodhound's. He strutted out of the saloon and mounted his horse.

Clackson turned to Poker Dines. 'There are moments when you have to show who is still the boss around here, eh?'

'Rick will be facing seven of 'em. Mean and thick as thieves. If he starts talking about arresting two of 'em, things might turn nasty.'

'You are saying, Poker, the sheriff might not return?'

'That's possible.'

'It's how I figured it,' smirked Clackson. 'I know you've been doing all Sully's dirty work for months, now. Maybe, you deserve to be this town's next lawman.'

'Well, I reckon I've always been loyal to Rick, but I admit he's losing his grip, lately.'

'I'll tell you what you have to do to win the sheriff's star. Sam Cotter's a nuisance. Get rid of him! Then make sure Ben Wild has killed off Chip Ross;

if it isn't done by now, you shoot them both.'

'That's a lot of killing.'

'If I settle your gambling debts, Poker, I reckon we'll be square, eh?'

7

Despite his objections, Sully rode hard through the night. He lashed his horse unmercifully, not to get the utmost speed out of the animal, but it satisfied his cruel temper to take his venom out on something that couldn't hit back. It wasn't a perilous ride. The moon was bright and although it flirted with the clouds, the shadows merely danced across the wide track.

He reached the outlaws' hide-out in two hours, a derelict bunkhouse on an abandoned ranch, and the clatter of horse's hoofs brought a surly guard to his feet. Sully barged into the bunkhouse, ignoring the man outside the door. The stench inside was vile enough to rock him back on his heels. Unwashed men set up a thick fug with the smoke from their cheap cigars. Food lay on plates at the mercy of insects, the dirt floor was littered with rubbish. Sully knew they couldn't agree on anything, especially housework. That was a woman's work and, as there wasn't one about the place, washing-up and sweeping the floor and airing the blankets never got done. Sully had always been their leader, the brains of the outfit who planned the bank raids and the cattle rustling in the days before he was given the job of town sheriff. But he had never deserted his gang and employed them as his regular posse. Now, his anger against Clackson was so furious he had other ideas.

Six men were playing poker at the long table, swigging whisky and chain-smoking. They were dull and lazy. If Sully had wanted to he could have created carnage with six shots before the outlaws blinked. As it was, the card players took a couple of minutes to become aware of their intruder.

'Rick! What you want this time o' night?' asked Butch, one of the men Sully had been sent to arrest.

'Kill the game,' snapped Sully.

'Hey! I got a good hand!' protested Max.

He was the thug who had come close to raping Dee. Sully showed he meant business by drawing a revolver and covering the men at the table. They stared at him stunned and frightened. A weak lot, thought Sully, and wondered if he shouldn't make a clean break and go solo. 'Slide your guns to this end of the table,' he ordered.

'What's this all about?' demanded Butch.

There was a chorus of protests as the outlaws refused to give up their guns, and the fact that he was disobeyed increased Sully's anger. He had to be convinced they still wanted him as their leader. There had been much dissent after the hard, gruelling ride, empty-handed from Camp Waterfall. In the days of their bank raids and cattle rustling there was always something to show for their efforts.

'I've been instructed to arrest Butch

and Max and take you in to Hometown.'

'I've done nothing,' said Max.

'You assaulted the most popular girl
in town. Dee can't talk or sing and
that's cost Hoot Clackson a lot of
dough.'

'A bit of horseplay, that's all it was.'

'Tell the locals that at your trial. I can
see a lynching taking place.'

'Sully, you ain't taking us in,' said
Butch.

'We're six guns, Rick. We can bore
you full of holes . . . ' threatened Max.

'Not before I take most of you with
me,' snapped Sully.

There followed a tense pause.
Nobody made a reckless move that
would start a gunfight. The six outlaws
obviously outnumbered the sheriff, but
they knew how accurate a shot he was,
and his gun was in his fist, while they
still had to draw.

'Truth is,' said Max, 'we ain't getting
much out of being honest. We been
villains all our lives and working on the

side of the law ain't to our liking.'

Suddenly, Sully put his gun away and sneered at them. 'Yeller bellies, I knew too well you wouldn't draw a gun on me.'

His mob fidgeted with their hands, shuffling cards and stirring coins. They wore foolish grins that hid their relief. 'We all knew you were only joking!'

Sully tightened his fat lips in his familiar cruel smile. 'Don't ever be sure about me. Nobody knows which way this cat jumps. I said I'd been ordered to arrest Butch and Max. When was the last time I took orders from anyone? I didn't say I was going to do it.'

He slumped into a chair at the table. His nose wrinkled in distaste at the outlaws' presence. 'You lot live like pigs.'

'There ain't going to be any arrests, eh, Rick?'

'No, Max. In fact, I'm quitting being sheriff.'

'You mean, it'll be like old times?'

'If you boys want it to be.'

'We're with you, Rick.'

'Then we get out of here in the morning and ride south.'

★　★　★

The distant sound of a bugle sounding reveille stirred Sam from sleep on the hard floor of the stables. He put on his boots and was glad to get out in the fresh air of a fine daybreak. He'd been grateful for the free bed, but the odour of musty hay and damp straw, together with the hot breaths of the half-dozen horses Anvil Smith kept locked up, was something he found too oppressing.

He harnessed Taffy to the buggy, reflecting it seemed ages since he'd set out on an urgent mission to fetch a doctor, and set off on his return journey, feeling dismal because he had failed to persuade Doc Turner to accompany him.

Hometown was silent and deserted and it wasn't till he skirted the fifteen-acre field where the cavalry detachment were camped did the thunder from a hundred horses' hoofs vibrate beneath him. Taffy pricked up his ears and trotted forward uneasily. The buggy slowed and gave Sam the opportunity of watching the men in dark-blue and gold uniforms at drill. The major, who had showed his dislike of Sam, was at the head of his column. With sword drawn he charged frantically across the open space of the field, and then suddenly shouted to his men to draw their sabres. 'Charge! Let's cut these red heathens to pieces!'

The cavalry screamed in a chorus, so fanatical it was difficult to believe they were only on a mock exercise, but Sam was convinced the hatred and the determination to slaughter the Indians, agitated by the formidable major, was displayed by every one of the hundred troopers. The noise swept across the camp and bounced back in an echo that made Sam realize if ever the army was given orders to shift the Crow tribe from the land it occupied north of Chip

Ross's spread, the blood would flow freely.

Sam urged Taffy into a canter and they left the army camp at speed, rounding the field and heading for the main trail out of town.

He pulled up outside the sheriff's office and went in to collect his guns. A bleary-eyed Poker Dines sprawled over the littered desk, but there was no sign of Sully. Sam made no enquiries. Poker handed over the guns. 'Early bird, ain't you?' he grunted.

'Nothing to keep me in this town.'

'That's smart. Where you heading for?'

'Camp Waterfall.'

'Take the old Sioux trail,' suggested Poker, with unusual politeness.

'Thanks,' mused Sam innocently.

He climbed into the buggy and set off. Taffy was fresh and eager and they made good speed while the sun hadn't yet moved overhead. The trail was wide and flat and without bends. It was isolated territory with only the range of hills on Sam's left to break up the monotonous countryside. Sam halted the buggy frequently to rest Taffy. Watering places and thick lush pasture were not difficult to find while shelter beneath willow trees that bowed above lively, clear streams were strangely peaceful in such a lawless country.

Taffy strode out nobly and the whirring of the buggy wheels made a pleasant sound but, after they had covered a further two miles, Sam detected a foreign noise that had nothing to do with Taffy's hoofs or the sweet-moving buggy. Sam turned in his seat. A cloud of dust hung low to the ground, moving fast in his wake. A horseman pursued him at a furious speed. A slim, lightweight rider on a powerful, long-striding Quarter Horse was more than a match for a young mustang hauling a buggy, and was covering so much ground in his pursuit, Sam readily recognized the thin, aggressive features of the deputy sheriff, Poker Dines. It did not occur to Sam immediately that he was being hunted down till a bullet whined across the open plains and kicked up the dust, yards wide of the buggy. 'Why me?' muttered Sam breathlessly.

What he did know, however, was that he'd behaved like a greenhorn by divulging to Poker his destination, and then stupidly accepting Poker's suggestion of the route to take. He'd played right into the hands of the crooked lawman.

A second shot shaved his large hat and two more explosions from Poker's gun caused Taffy to rear in fright. It was the first time the plucky horse had been under fire, and the echoes sounded louder than the original noise in the way they struck the surrounding hills and vibrated across the flat land.

Sam fought to regain control of the horse. 'Easy, Taffy. We got to get out of this. Damn me, I quit his precious town when he told me to. What else does he want?'

Taffy landed evenly and Sam steered

him on a zig-zag course along the trail. The horse seemed to get the idea of how to avoid the bullets, and he not only swung wide to make Poker's aim more difficult, but he galloped at a speed quite unique for a small horse. Sam felt he'd trained a wonder horse and the distance between the buggy and the pursuer widened, while at the same time, the zig-zag course confused Poker.

Sam decided it would be a contest to which horse controlled the most stamina. His young mustang was big-hearted and loved to race, but wasn't bred for galloping over long distances. Poker's steed was fast, and over a quarter of a mile could beat any horse in the country. It was where the Quarter Horse got his name from. Sam wondered how much stamina Poker's horse would have left after the initial sprint.

But hauling the buggy was always a handicap to the gallant Taffy and Poker began to close the gap between them again. Despite making the target more difficult by the erratic course Sam steered, he was now well in range from Poker's shots, who by skilful riding without the use of his hands was able to fire both of his revolvers at the same time. Sam swept to and fro in wide circles to avoid the bullets and, while the frantic Taffy swung the buggy wildly, often on one wheel, it was impossible for Sam to use his own guns and return the shots when he needed all his concentration on controlling the horse.

The deadly chase went on. Sam was soaked with perspiration and he could see no end to the arid plains. His hands slipped on the leather reins and he felt that Taffy would run till he dropped from exhaustion. The small horse was lathered with sweat and the zig-zag course he followed meant he was covering far more distance than if he travelled in a straight line.

Poker closed in, firing incessantly, but wasting bullets. Yellow dust rose thickly in the shimmering heat. For one moment, Sam was in a direct line to his pursuer and he presented a sitting target. Poker aimed carefully. The drumming of horses' hoofs were deafening in Sam's ears. He pulled hard on his left rein, expecting Taffy to veer away from the straight line he was on, but the mustang had given everything he had. The horse stumbled and coughed, then sank to his knees whinnying pitifully. Sam was thrown forward from his seat, lost his balance and crashed to the ground. He twisted away from the spinning wheels of the buggy and lay flat on his stomach, breathing hard to calm himself. Nearby, Taffy panted unevenly, but remained conscious. Sam found cover beneath the buggy, the crash had been so sudden it robbed Poker of a perfect shot and he held his fire. The ground vibrated beneath Sam as if an earthquake was imminent. He drew his guns and waited for Poker to make the next move. His eyes grew enormous with amazement for suddenly the fight had become a three-cornered contest. The speed of Poker's horse took it past the fallen buggy and the lawman now faced a young Crow buck, riding his Morgan horse from the opposite direction. The Indian emerged from the heavy dust cloud as if he'd dropped from the skies and screaming a war-cry he took Poker by complete surprise. Poker's hands froze on his guns and the fury on the Crow's face petrified the lawman. Sam heard the whirring sound of an arrow speeding through the air and he switched his gaze to the young buck. By the time the arrow had plunged into Poker's chest, the Crow had fixed a second arrow into his bow and fired. The second arrow pierced Poker's throat. He uttered a final gurgle and collapsed on his horse. The Crow rode swiftly to the side of Poker's horse and deftly removed the guns from Poker's hands and thrust them in the top of his buckskin trousers. Then he gave Poker's horse a hard slap. The horse took off, heading for the direction he knew best, back to Hometown carrying his dead owner with him.

It was all over in seconds. Sam was confused. Poker had been out to kill him, so he wasn't sorry the Indian had intervened, but he couldn't be certain it was a rescue act because this was the Crow buck who had stolen the Morgan horse Sam had hired from Anvil Smith. Sam had the opportunity to shoot the Indian. It would have been ungrateful since the Indian had saved his life, and what would the repercussions be if the Indian was found shot? A full-scale rising against the white man?

Oddly enough, the Indian took scant interest in Sam, lying prone under the buggy. Instead, he faced the hills and threw his fists into the air.

'I am Silent Hunter and from this moment I have completed the rites that enrols me as a warrior in the Crow tribe, the bravest fighters of them all. I have stolen my enemy's horse, and his guns and have struck him down.'

After declaring his achievement, Silent Hunter rode away. Sam climbed out from beneath the buggy, and stood staring at the new, young warrior. He wasn't sure if he should bless the Crow or curse himself for wasting the chance of retrieving the stolen Morgan horse. He realized, no matter how strong and determined Silent Hunter had proved himself to be, the Morgan horse had to be recaptured and returned to his rightful owner, irrespective if stealing it had satisfied one of the rites necessary to enrol the young Crow buck into warrior status.

Sam examined the exhausted Taffy, got him to his feet and walked the horse in gentle fashion until he was satisfied there was no lameness. He found a shallow stream and bathed Taffy's swollen limbs then allowed the horse to rest for the remainder of the day. It meant losing several hours and he could imagine Chip fretting over the time it had taken him to complete the journey.

The following morning, Taffy was

eager and fresh. Sam harnessed him to the buggy and they set off at a lively pace. By late afternoon Camp Waterfall was sighted, the sun gleaming on the long, winding river and golden reflections dancing in a circle on the whirlpool beneath the glinting waterfall.

At approximately the same time, a lone horse jogged into Hometown, the rider slumped across the animal's back like a sack of corn. A trooper, belonging to the cavalry detachment, was off-duty when the weary horse attracted the attention of the locals. The trooper caught the horse. The corpse was immediately recognized as Poker Dines and the two arrows embedded in his body were recognized by their feathers as belonging to the Crow tribe.

The trooper raced back to camp to report the incident to his major.

'Those Indian scum are killing white men, eh? I think the moment is ripe to teach the Crow tribe a lesson,' decided Major Rod Ross, with an excited gleam in his eyes.

8

Sam pulled up outside the ranch-house and jumped down from the buggy. He fully expected his arrival to have brought an anxious Chip striding from the house, or if not Chip, one of the Indian boys who worked either in the stables or the kitchen. 'Hello! I'm here!' he announced.

His voice sounded hollow and the echoes pranced in between the cluster of out-houses, but there was no response. He quickly took care of Taffy, releasing him from the buggy and putting him to graze on a stretch of lush grass.

He hurried into the house, going from room to room. The emptiness haunted him and suddenly he thought of the young, ambitious gunman, Ben Wild. Sam had taken it for granted he'd see no more of the arrogant youth when

150

he was handed over to Sully in exchange for the Indian trader, Nickel Joe.

Sully had resented young Ben being employed by Hoot Clackson to kill Chip. Assassinations were the lawman's speciality, but they cost a lot of dollars. Ben Wild was a gunman on the cheap and for fifty dollars Hoot Clackson hoped to get rid of Chip, so that his land would become vacant for Clackson to buy and then resell to the railway barons. Ben was a nuisance to Sully and Sam was convinced the gunman would vanish once in the hands of the cruel and crooked sheriff. But what if Ben was still at large and trusted to carry out his original assignment? What if he'd already taken Chip by surprise and in the subsequent shoot-out had accounted for the horse-breeder and every-one in the house? That would include Dee and the two Indian house boys.

He searched every room except the bedroom allocated to the sick Dee. He knocked on the door and called her name, didn't wait for a reply, but burst into the room, then pulled up at the foot of the bed in shock.

He found himself looking at a very sick young woman. Dee was thin and her complexion yellow. The beautiful auburn hair, she was noted for, looked like a pile of rusty metal. There was no life in her eyes and only a few people, who knew her well, could have distinguished her from the rare, young beauty who captivated the local audiences in Hometown's centre of entertainment. Sam touched her cold hand and but for a slight flicker of her pale lips he could have mistaken her for being dead. He spoke softly to her. 'Dee, where is Chip?'

She could not answer him. The bruises on her throat had turned a deep purple, but her physical injuries were not so important as her lack of nourishment. Sam could see she was starving or dying of thirst and he wondered how long she'd been left here alone.

He poured water into a glass and put the glass to her lips. She lapped the water like a greedy pup, but the pain of trying to swallow the water made her gasp and heave. She was immediately sick.

Sam bathed her face and arms to bring coolness to her feverish body, but there was nothing else he could do without a doctor. He wished now he'd forced Doc Turner at pistol-point to accompany him. He turned to leave the room. Dee moaned painfully, fearful of being left on her own again.

'I'll be back soon,' he promised her.

He almost ran from the room. It sickened him to see Dee in such a terrible state and he couldn't put his anger aside that it was possible she'd been cruelly abandoned. Perhaps, it was normal behaviour in this callous country.

He dashed out of the house and without bothering to saddle Taffy he leaped on his bare back and rode him across the river to the neighbour's sheep farm. A pair of shepherds, rifles resting across their knees, dozed beneath their wide Mexican hats, while a flock of sheep grazed on a square pasture, content with the evening sun on their backs. Sam rode up to them. One of the shepherds opened his eyes and gripped his rifle. 'Yeah, what you want?'

'I'm looking for Chip Ross?'

'Ain't seen him all day.'

Sam reflected guiltily he'd been away from Camp Waterfall for more than four and a half days. 'If not today, what about yesterday or when did you last see him?'

'Can't rightly say, son.'

Sam was about to wheel his horse, impatient at the blank answers he'd received from the dim-witted sheep-man, when he looked down sharply at the grubby man. 'Has there been any shooting about here, lately?'

'Shooting?' squinted the shepherd.

Sam wasn't altogether sure he hadn't struck at the truth. 'You know, gun-play.'

'Ain't heard anything like a shot.'

'Seen any strangers?'

'Not since the night that sheriff and his posse took over our bunkhouse. They left this kid behind when they left.'

'Was his name Ben?'

'Aye, I reckon it was. Cocky young varmint. Always boasting about being a gunfighter.'

'Where is he now?'

'Dunno. He took his bedding-roll and his guns and quit.'

'Have you seen him since?'

'Nope.'

'If you do come across him, don't say I'm looking for him.'

'Can't very well if I don't know who you might be.'

'Just as well, then,' said Sam and continued his search.

The only other habitation in the territory was the Crow lodge, north of the river. Sam had been there, but only in the company of Chip, the Indians' trusted friend. It was a dangerous mission for a white man, especially as Sam considered himself a stranger, to venture alone into Indian territory but the Crow warriors probably knew more about Chip's movements than did his lethargic neighbours. He rode hard towards the hills that overlooked the long avenue of tepees, the gaily painted, conical tents fashioned from animal skins. He was convinced he was being watched as he took the narrow trail towards the foothills. The Crow tribe were fighters and always prepared for unexpected attacks, so they posted scouts on the high ground and if any strangers approached they warned the warriors in the lodge, either by signalling with mirrors when the sun was high or sending fleet-footed runners with verbal messages.

It was the time of day when the tribe was the least active and most of the Indians had retired to their tepees to pursue their traditional artwork of painting, embroidery and needlework. Sam advanced cautiously, the mustang picking his way over the rough cobbles of the track, and although the lodge appeared deserted, Sam had been spied upon when he was still half a mile from the outskirts of the Crow settlement.

By the time he crossed the boundary between Chip's spread and the Indian territory, fifty warriors had assembled in the clearing outside the tepees, fully armed with bows and arrows and wicked-looking, long, hunting knives. Some held stone-headed clubs, swinging them menacingly, their eyes never departing from the lone rider. Others leaned on tall spears. Sam's initial uneasiness turned to real fear. His face dripped with perspiration and his whole body felt clammy, while his mind suddenly went blank as he scanned the hostile faces. Then, with military precision the warriors moved forward. Taffy was grabbed by the halter and Sam found he was surrounded. He was tongue-tied, trembling at the thought of what horrors the tribe would put him through. His past life swept before his eyes and it bewildered him to think how an English stable-lad could end up being threatened by redskins in this strange, vast, new country.

The warriors began to chant a war-cry and their feet beat out a tempo which drummed on the hard ground. The echo travelled along the avenue of tepees and as the warriors grew more excited they lifted their voices in a chorus of triumphant shouting. Sam's hands and feet were bound with cord. Weapons were raised aloft and amid savage cheers the orders went out: 'To the ant hills with him!'

Sam watched them gather wood to stake him to the ground. 'I am friend of Chip Ross,' he protested weakly.

They either did not understand him or chose to ignore his cry. The long, noisy procession moved forward but, when it reached the last tepee before fanning out into open country, the wide flap of the tepee was unhitched and a neat, slender Crow maiden, her lovely, dark eyes full of indignation, positioned herself in the opening. She was dressed simply in a short buckskin skirt and a cotton blouse. Her black hair was shorn severely and parted in the middle, leaving her beautiful features framed in an oval face. She folded her bare arms across her chest, pursed her lips and the fire in her expression trapped the leading warrior and he faltered in his triumphant march. Sam knew nothing about the tribe, but he was certain the beautiful squaw was not the daughter of a chief or held any high position in the tribe, yet her authority was undeniable. The warriors were nervous of her and when she spoke, she silenced them at a stroke.

'What is all this vulgar commotion about? Don't you know I have a score of sick children here?'

'We are sorry for the noise, Gentle Sunrise, but it is many moons ago when we held prisoner a white man.'

The Indian girl's eyes blazed at the leading warrior. 'What is the use of my work with medicine if you continue your barbaric methods of killing your enemies? Who is he?'

The crowd parted and allowed Sam to have a complete view of Gentle Sunrise. His weakness for pretty girls in this moment was almost suffocating. He smiled bravely and for the first time since he'd trespassed into the Crow territory his brain started to work to his advantage. He leaned forward on his horse and regarded the young medicine woman with an eagerness that might help him wriggle out of his terrifying predicament. 'I came searching for Chip Ross. He's gone missing.'

Gentle Sunrise knew enough of the English language to understand what Sam told her, although his dialect puzzled her. She turned furiously upon the gathering of warriors and swore at them in their own language. Her cursing reduced them to embarrassed expressions and there was much fidgeting with their weapons. The leading warrior stared sheepishly at Sam.

'You ignorant fools! Untie him. Don't

you recognize him as Chip's friend? Didn't he come to the lodge a week ago and save Nickel Joe's life, and would we still be settled here if it wasn't for Chip? Have you such poor memories that you forget the sheriff from Hometown ordered us to move on?'

Sam held out his bound hands and while one warrior cut the cords, another released his bound feet. The medicine woman smiled tenderly up at him. 'My people will remember you in future. You are always welcome, but I'm sorry I haven't seen Chip for days. My work keeps me confined to the lodge.'

'If you are skilled with medicine will you help me?'

'The Crow tribe has always been famous for their knowledge of herbal cures and nature's medicines and I have been taught how to treat the sick. Even our enemies bring sick children to me for my reputation makes me sought after far and wide.'

'Will you come with me, please? Chip Ross has a woman who is dying.'

Sam didn't have to plead. Anyone belonging to the Crow tribe would have sacrificed their life for Chip. He was the sole honest white man who protected their interests against land-grabbers like Hoot Clackson.

Gentle Sunrise darted into her tepee and returned with a large bag, bulging with medicines. 'You see what time you have wasted? Is this your way of repaying our best friend? Bring me a pony, pronto!' she stormed at the assembly.

A moment later she was riding with Sam to Chip's ranch-house. There was still no sign of Chip or the Indian houseboys, and when Sam showed her into Dee's bedroom, the alarm on the medicine woman's face could not be disguised.

Dee's revulsion for all Indians was not aroused. She was too far gone to object to the cool, skilful hands examining her and she slept totally exhausted, not knowing who it was Sam had brought to save her life.

'If she does not drink soon she will die, and she is in great pain with fever.'

'I gave her a drink of water, but she couldn't take it,' said Sam.

'You must collect empty bottles and ride to the waterfall. That is the purest water to be found anywhere. It has curing properties. You must bring back as much water as you can carry. Also, you do know the white willow tree?'

'I know it.'

'Then scrape pieces of the willow bark from the tree. I will crush it into a powder and give a little of it to the sick woman. She will not feel so much pain and the swelling of her throat will go down. Then she can eat.'

Sam went to the stables. Chip wasn't a whisky-drinking man and empty bottles were few and far between, but there were saddle-bags and canvas water canteens hanging from the rafters that Chip used on his long periods away from his spread during the round-up months and drives to the horse fairs.

Sam grabbed all the containers there

163

were and strapped them to Taffy, then with just enough good light to see him safely along the banks of the broad, shining river he rode out to the waterfall. He took a soaking, perched on the slippery rocks, while collecting the icy water in the canteens, then he put the canteens into the saddle-bags. A cluster of white willow trees bowed over the river. Sam had tethered his horse to one of the trees. A fine moon escaped from the gathering gloom of the night sky and filtered through the branches. He packed the saddlebags on to the horse and was ready to ride home when he stared rather amused at the willow tree. He could only accept Gentle Sunrise's claim as being traditional Crow folklore. Maybe chewing the tree bark to relieve pain was all-right for Indians, but the white man knew nothing of such medicine. He did believe, however, in the healing qualities of the pure spring water. In his native country there was a town called Tunbridge Wells where the rich 'took the waters' to cure all kinds of ills. He hesitated again. The young Crow doctor was such a determined woman that to ignore her instructions might bring her fiery wrath upon him, so he took his hunting knife and sliced strips of bark from the tree. The bark oozed a white juice and he wondered if the juice wasn't the magic pain killer. He packed the strips of bark into his saddle-bag and suddenly conscious that he'd taken too long over his mission he rode Taffy in a furious gallop home to Chip's spread.

He dismounted and then saw the Morgan horse that Silent Hunter, the newly fledged warrior had stolen from him, hitched to a post close to the house.

Sam collected the canteens of water and the saddle-bag containing the strips of bark and strode into the room where Gentle Sunrise was keeping an intense vigil over the sick Dee, despite the angry interruptions from the young warrior.

'You are such a jealous fool!' the Crow girl stormed at the young warrior. 'Can't you see why I have come to the white man's house?'

'It isn't right you are here alone with Chip Ross.'

'Chip isn't here. He's gone missing along with his two Indian boys. I'm here to cure this sick woman.'

Sam decided it was time to barge in and cut short the argument between the couple. He handed over the medicines which the Crow girl accepted gratefully, while Silent Hunter watched with sullen eyes and pouting lips. Suddenly, he beat his bare chest with his huge fists. 'I am warrior now that I have performed the tribal rites and I claim you, Gentle Sunrise, as my woman. You come with me, now!'

'You can visit the burial ground of your forefathers before I leave a sick patient,' retorted the Crow girl.

She turned her back on the ill-tempered Silent Hunter and persuaded Dee to take sips of the clear, ice-cold spring water. Dee licked her swollen lips and gasped for more. She drank and her eyes flickered, then Gentle Sunrise crushed a piece of the tree bark into a fine powder and placed it on Dee's tongue and followed it by giving the sick woman sips of the sparkling water. The treatment seemed to be working, but Silent Hunter continued to be a constant nuisance and threatened to upset the Crow doctor's concentration.

In desperation she turned upon the young warrior and snapped, 'For the sake of my patient and my own health go outside.'

Sam suddenly hit upon an idea that would remove the nuisance. He faced the Crow warrior squarely in his bronzed features and said calmly, 'That Morgan saddle horse you stole from me belongs to the smithy in Hometown. I'll fight you to win it back.'

Silent Hunter could not, dare not, refuse the challenge, especially with his woman as a witness to it. He nodded grimly and said, 'We fight for the horse.'

The two men strode out of the room, leaving the young Crow girl to tend to the sick Dee without further interruption. Outside on the cobbled yard the moonlight beamed from above the surrounding hills and spread a bright yellow carpet between the outhouses. Silent Hunter, always eager to prove his prowess, jumped into an aggressive stance. Features scowling in a savage expression, his lithe body arched and knees braced, the long hunting knife was already glinting from his right hand. Sam gave him a puzzled frown and instantly threw his own knife to the ground. 'We can fight for the horse without either of us being killed,' he said and put up his fists for his own protection.

Bare-fist fighting wasn't the Crow way to settle differences. The white man fought that way when they'd swallowed too much firewater but, to the Indian, fighting without weapons was like a couple of squaws scrapping, biting and scratching at each other. Silent Hunter was immediately shamed by Sam's willingness to take him on with or without a knife and the matter was soon resolved by Sam's fierce left-hand punch that landed high on the warrior's shoulder. The blow had the effect of paralyzing the whole arm and hand and the warrior's knife clattered to the ground. While at a disadvantage, his right arm hanging loosely by his side, the warrior backed away. Sam pounced with feet dancing and fists pounding; punching hard and accurately, he soon had the bemused Indian cornered between the big barn and the tool shed. In sheer desperation Silent Hunter raised his legs in a high kicking defence and caught Sam on the jaw. Sam rocked back on his heels and was not surprised when the Indian charged at him employing all the rough and dirty tactics never permitted in the noble art of boxing. Sam was head-butted in the stomach, the warrior's long fingernails tore into his face, and his ears were bitten and his long hair pulled savagely. Sam back-pedalled hastily, throwing long-range punches, scoring heavily, then side-stepping and crashing left and right hooks into the warrior's face. Silent Hunter's arms reached out, like twin venomous snakes, and he tried to wrestle his opponent, grabbing at Sam's throat in an attempt to strangle him. Sam slipped beneath the menacing arms and beat a two-fisted drumming against the warrior's naked, lean stomach. Silent Hunter was forced into the open. He looked a sorry sight with cut lips and bruised body. He was panting breathlessly, aware that he couldn't match the white man's skill, and only his brave spirit kept him in the fight. Sam gave silent thanks to the ex-pug, who had taught him back in England, how to use his fists, and then waded into the warrior to finish him off with a flurry of blows.

Silent Hunter crashed to the ground, the impact of his head hitting the cobbles laid him unconscious for a full minute. When he finally opened his eyes, the moon had climbed high above the hills and blinded him. He only saw a vague outline of Sam bending over him.

'Enough?' asked Sam.

The defeated warrior grunted his agreement. 'The horse is yours.'

'I shall return it to the rightful owner,' said Sam, and helped the fallen man to his feet.

Their eyes met out of scarred faces, then suddenly, the heat of the battle was over and they exchanged broad grins. Silent Hunter embraced Sam and adopted him as his brother. 'We will hunt, track and fight together.'

Sam wasn't certain if he wanted to be a member of the Crow tribe, but the young warrior would be a better friend than enemy. 'I'll be happy to hunt with you.'

The pleasant exchanges would have gone on longer if it hadn't been for the anguished cry from Gentle Sunrise. She stood in the doorway of the house, a grimy, crumpled piece of paper clutched in her hand. 'Dee has remembered. A young gunman came and took Chip and the two Indian boys away at gunpoint. The gunman left a ransom note under Dee's pillow.'

9

Sam read the ransom note, his lips curled cynically. 'So, Ben Wild had got ambitious. He figures Chip Ross is worth more than the fifty dollars Hoot Clackson paid him to kill him. He's demanding two hundred dollars before he lets him go.'

'Where is Ben Wild holding them? I hope the Indian boys are included in the deal,' asked Dee, her voice frail, the fever still high and bringing out beads of pespiration on her thin face.

'Some place called Thunder Gorge.'

'I know it!' cried Silent Hunter fingering his long hunting knife. 'We go and hunt down this dog.'

He was so eager for the action he hoisted his bow and score of arrows on to his back and strode to the door.

'Not so fast,' Sam called out to him. 'It is already dead of night.'

'There is a fine moon to light our path. Let us hunt when the prey least expects us.'

Sam nodded warily. It was heartening to know he would have the Crow warrior as his accomplice and tracker in this wild territory and, as for Ben Wild's demand, he could sing for that till the sheep came home. Two hundred dollars! Sam hadn't got two cents.

Dee stirred and raised herself in the bed despite Gentle Sunrise's restraining hand. 'Wait! There is no need for bloodshed. You will find enough dollars in my bag. Pay off Ben Wild.'

Sam scowled rebelliously. 'Kow-tow to that cur. What the hell!'

'It's my money, Sam. I want Chip freed and back here with me at any cost.'

'You have always refused to share his roof before.'

'I was wrong to think I'm better than an Indian. Gentle Sunrise has saved my life. I haven't the desire to go back on the music-hall stage and if I can help

Chip look after the Crow tribe's welfare, that is what I want to do. But bring Chip and his Indian boys back safely.'

Sam reluctantly helped himself to the money in Dee's travelling-bag. He glanced at Dee and managed to swallow his pride, but said, 'I can whip Ben Wild anytime.'

'Not this time, Sam. We need Chip here.'

Despite his aversion to guns, Sam checked his gunbelt was full of shells and his revolvers were clean. He'd got as much trust in Ben Wild as he had in a rattlesnake.

'The journey to the gorge is many hours long. We need horses,' said Silent Hunter.

Sam thought of what amusement Ben had treated himself to while holding his prisoners. He doubted if they would be in any condition to walk for a long distance. 'You can ride the Morgan, and I'll take Taffy. We'll borrow a pair of Chip's strong pack-horses.'

'Sounds like a procession to me,' Gentle Sunrise said doubtfully.

'Thunder Gorge has the echoes of a thousand ghosts. It will be impossible to hide our approach. This mission will be dangerous,' admitted Silent Hunter.

He spoke with relish and winked broadly at Sam as they left the house and crossed the moonlit yard to collect the horses. The Crow warrior led the way, guiding the Morgan saddle-horse along virgin tracks and keeping the gaunt range of hills to his left. Despite the tracks twisting across a barren valley, strewn with granite rocks, Silent Hunter kept the hills in view. They rode for three hours mostly at a walking pace and when they reached the gaping entrance to the gorge, Sam realized why it was called Thunder Gorge. Although the horses moved at a gentle pace the hoofs drummed against the high rock walls and the echoes bounced to and fro in a startling noise. The grey dust rose from the ground and caught the horses' nostrils and when they sneezed it sounded like a violent explosion. Silent Hunter dismounted and looked up at Sam. 'From here I will go my own way.'

Sam didn't protest. The ransom note made special mention that he should come to Thunder Gorge alone, but he wasn't against sharing elusive tactics with the Crow warrior.

'I know tracks in these parts where no man has walked before. Maybe we can surprise this cocky gunman,' said the Indian.

Sam was all for a bit of trickery. He'd been against handing over the money in the first place. 'I'll take care of the horses.'

Silent Hunter pointed to a spot several hundred yards further along the gorge where the huge rocks overhung the narrow passage. 'There is a cave there. I guess it is the only shelter where a man can hold his prisoners. Tread carefully, my friend, and keep your hands on your guns.'

Sam watched the Crow warrior scale

the rocks overhead, admiring the ease with which he climbed and was quite mystified when the Indian vanished from view within minutes.

Sam went forward, riding Taffy and trailing the trio of horses, in and out of the deep shadows, but his approach was less then silent. He reached the mouth of the cave. The opening yawned darkly in front of him, and there was no sound from within. He dismounted and abandoned the horses. With a gun in each hand he crept forward. The darkness of the cave hit him as if he was blind and he would have sworn Silent Hunter was wrong about the site where Chip and the two Indian boys were held hostage if it hadn't been for the painful moan that drifted towards him.

At the far end of the cave a crevice allowed a shaft of silver moonlight to lighten the way. It fell upon three hunched figures slumped against the wet walls of the cave, where the spring water flowed from the hills and dripped through the roof of the cave.

The prisoners were in a sorry state. Bound hand and foot, the cuts and bruises on their punched faces, the hollow cheeks and staring eyes told how Ben Wild had roughly handled them. Their low moans and constant coughing was evident of their weakness and Sam doubted if they had eaten or quenched their thirsts since being captured. Sam's fury reached limits that he was unable to control. The hands that gripped the guns shook. Sweat poured down his face and he was too eager to let Chip know of his presence. He became too confident and darted forward to release the trio. 'Chip! It's Sam!'

He barely heard the scuffle behind him, but the revolver prodding the middle of his back was prominent enough to tell him of his carelessness and Ben Wild's sneering voice haunted him. 'You been a long time coming, Sam Cotter.'

'The dollars weren't easy to raise.'

'Got 'em now?'

'In my inside pocket.'

'Don't turn round. Drop your guns and put the dollars on the floor.'

'I'll hand over my guns, but you set free the prisoners before you get the dollars.'

'You've always taken me for a fool, Sam Cotter. Well, you got no room to argue.'

Sam feared, what he'd learned since he'd landed from England, the American double-cross. 'What's the game, Ben Wild?'

'No game. Just get over on that wall with your pals. I'll help myself to some target practice.'

Sam lurched forward. 'You'd shoot us down like dogs, in cold blood? Give me a chance. You've always fancied yourself as a gunman. Take me on, eh!'

'Professional gunmen take no chances. Get against that wall.'

'You're a butcher, Ben Wild.'

Sam took two paces towards the wall. It left a gap between him and Ben. The sadistic gunman was isolated. From the narrow crevice at the far end of the cave the tip of an arrow glinted in the moonlight. Ben Wild held his guns at hip level, his trigger fingers ready to squeeze, an amused grin on his boyish face.

An arrow winged its flight on an accurate and deady path. Silent and devastating the missile hardly disturbed the air in the dark cave. It struck Ben Wild in the throat, paralyzing his whole body. The two guns dropped to the ground and the victim fell stiffly without a sound. Sam looked towards the crevice in the back entrance to the cave, which Silent Hunter had located. The Crow warrior was squeezing his lithe body through and with a triumphant shout joined the stunned Sam, who stood and stared at the dead Ben Wild.

Sam was numbed, speechless. Seconds away from being shot down in cold blood along with Chip and the two Indian boys, his potential killer now lay at his feet. 'What you call a bullseye, eh!' Silent Hunter cried.

He slapped Sam on the back, and although the warrior had saved his life, Sam failed to enthuse over the Indian's success. Sam had always been on the opposite side of the fence to Ben Wild, but in a strange sort of way he pitied him more than hated the arrogant young gunman, and if given the chance, Sam would have struck up a friendship with the city boy, showed him the uselessness of posing as a professional gunman and led him towards a safer and longer life. He shook his head sadly, sympathizing with Ben's wasted ambition, that only led to him being used by the crooked Hoot Clackson. 'Let's see to our friends,' he said solemnly.

Ben Wild's indifference to his prisoners, denying them food and water, hardened Sam's feelings towards the dead gunman. Once the trio were released and they sang the praises of their rescuers it was obvious not one of them could trust the mobility of his limbs. They were weak with hunger and needed a peaceful night's rest, but Chip was stubborn. His first thoughts were for Dee, frightened, sick and alone in the farmhouse. 'Damn it, Sam. If you've brought horses we'll get home.'

'You won't make it, Chip, and you don't have to worry about Dee. She's been well looked after and will soon be fit.'

'Give me a horse,' Chip demanded.

The two frail Indian boys, despite their unwavering loyalty towards Chip, could not summon enough strength to join their boss and they slid to the ground, content to be guided by Sam's wisdom. The determined Chip, however, staggered three paces towards the cave entrance, went limp and with a furious oath sprawled flat on his face. Angrily, he tried to climb to his feet, but hadn't the strength to respond to such an effort. Sam and Silent Hunter hauled him up. 'We'll build a fire,' Sam told him. 'We have brought food, water and blankets. You will eat and drink and have a good night's sleep. By noon you will be able to travel.'

Sam rustled up a meal of beans and coffee and by the warmth of the fire, utter fatigue and a full stomach soon sent them fast asleep. At daybreak, only Sam and Silent Hunter were awake. The Crow warrior went poaching for fresh meat and returned happily with a brace of fat rabbits. By noon, they all enjoyed a second meal, and despite his impatience to return to his spread, Chip was more cheerful and a healthy colour had returned to his bronzed, rugged features. His strapping, loose-limbed build soon allowed him to shake off the ordeal he'd suffered in the cave and when the party was ready to move off, he mounted a horse with one swift leap.

The two Indian boys were not so refreshed. They had to be helped up in the saddle of the docile pack-horses and rode with heads bowed and eyes half-shut with weariness.

Along the narrow gorge the heat was intense, the brilliant sun striking the granite walls and enclosing the single file of horsemen in a constant furnace. After an hour of sweating, with clothes sticking to their bodies, the horses moving sedately along the rocky track, they emerged from the gorge and halted to gaze upon the wide-open valley. A soft breeze drifted from the hilltop and felt cool on their backs. Silent Hunter was in the lead and from where he sat, surveying the landscape, his features suddenly took on an expression of savage intensity.

Sam guessed something was wrong in the manner Silent Warrior had reined in his horse so abruptly. He rode up front with Chip close behind him, and the trio stared into the valley, their throats dry and without speaking.

Beneath them, the long, winding column of army cavalry occupied the main track leading towards Camp Waterfall. It was a force of a hundred troops. Dark-blue uniforms with gold flashes gleamed in the sunshine. Sabres glinted as they swung from the saddles. Two scouts rode out in front dictating an easy, unhurried pace. The sight was impressive if the column was parading for some innocent rodeo show or military tattoo, but this column was equipped for a military operation. Horse-drawn wagons hauled tents and equipment, used for overnight camps during the advance from their Hometown base, while at the rear of the column four field guns and trailers trundled behind four pairs of army mules. At the head of the column, curtained by the United States and regimental flags, rode the splendid figure of the sabre-rattling major, whom Sam had seen exercise his men in a blood-curdling cavalry charge.

Now, on the final stage of their journey, they were ready for real action.

Chip chewed his lips thoughtfully. 'Those guys are going to war.'

'Hoot Clackson's behind this,' said Sam.

'He can't grab the land for the

railway barons other than by force,' muttered Chip.

'If they intend to wipe out my people,' said Silent Hunter, his mouth lined grimly, 'we will fight to the death. I promise you.'

It was precisely the threat Chip didn't want to hear. He'd worked hard to bring peace between the Crow tribe and the white man and the land they settled on together was a mark of the trust they had in each other. But that land was to be taken from them. The Crow tribe would fight to defend their settlement, which the army only saw as a squatters' camp. Chip would be paid off in railway dollars under a compulsory order from Washington.

What was he to do? Fight alongside the Indians against his own people or simply allow the army to trample all over him and what he'd built up during the past ten years when he'd bought the poor, derelict land at a dollar an acre?

The impulsive Silent Hunter had no time or temperament to be diplomatic, and without a word of explanation he whipped his horse into a gallop and rode furiously across the valley, raising clouds of yellow dust in his wake.

Chip peered towards the slow-moving army column. The sun reflected sharply on the glass of a pair of binoculars. 'Damn!' he swore, 'Silent Hunter has alerted them. I needed all the time I wanted.'

He turned and faced Sam. His thin face set like steel. 'I could pow-wow with that army major or the Crow chief and try and prevent the bloodshed.'

Sam shook his head doubtfully. 'That army major is a ruthless beast. He'll be desperate to get at the Indians.'

'And the Crow tribe are savage fighters,' mused Chip.

A faint echo of a man's crisp voice drifted towards them and the cavalry stepped up a pace. The jingle of harness and the grating of wheels made a sinister harmony. The cavalry were moving at the double. The troops whipping the horses into a charge.

'This isn't the time to stand and stare,' decided Chip.

He'd formed a plan of action and this wasn't the time for anyone to feel weak. It was a case of all hands to take part, and the two frail Indian boys, sprawled limply in the saddle were curtly ordered to get to the farmhouse. 'If we can persuade the Crow tribe to move down to my spread there's room in the house and the outbuildings. You boys move straw for mattresses and get in water and food. I can imagine the army laying siege to us if they feel cheated of a battle. Come on, Sam, let's see what speed you can get out of that mustang of yours and reach the Crow tribe before the cavalry does.'

The pair raced on ahead of the two Indian boys, across flat country and climbed the rise in the land that led towards the river bank. Chip headed for the shallow end of the broad river, roared his horse to charge to the top of the bank and then rode expertly down the slope into the water. Sam urged

Taffy to follow suit. The mustang, small and tireless, responded bravely and the two horses splashed their way to the opposite bank. Then it was uphill all the way to the Crow settlement. Chip stole a quick glance behind him. The cavalry remained in a column according to army discipline and their progress wasn't as fast as the two riders already within sight of the Crow camp.

Despite their furious ride, Chip and Sam found the Crow chief and his loyal warriors had gathered outside the chief's large and colourful tepee.

Silent Hunter's advance warning had inspired them to daub grotesque war paint on their faces. They were armed with all the weapons they could carry, bows and arrows, spears, hunting kives and stone-headed clubs. Chip could not feel anything but cynical. Crude weapons against field guns would prove a pathetic resistance.

'Chief, you won't stand a chance if you stay and fight the army.'

The chief was a huge, broad-chested

man with an evil grin. His confidence while surrounded by his hundred warriors was frightening. He looked as if he was spoiling for a fight and he pointed out to Chip how the camp was laid out in a defensive formation. The avenues between the tepees were so narrow they were difficult for a charging horse to negotiate and could only be ridden single file, while the tepees packed with warriors aiming their deadly arrows created a natural ambush.

Whatever tactics each side employed there was bound to be carnage.

'We fight to the death for what we believe is ours,' said the chief.

'It is obvious the army have orders to destroy your tribe and take over your land.'

'What about your land? Will you fight to save it?'

'I hope to talk peace, Chief.'

'If that fails will you fire your guns at your blood-brothers or will you support us?'

'No, I cannot fight the white man.'

'What are you doing here in the Crow camp then?'

'I want you and your people, your wives and children, your next generation to follow me. I will give you shelter and food.'

'And let the army take our land without a fight?'

'They will take it, with or without a fight.'

'Ha! And what happens afterwards when you have protected us from the army?'

'You must go to the hills and build a new settlement,' advised Chip.

'Where the land is barren and snow and ice make the ground impossible to farm? That is a poor exchange for our blood. We will stand and fight.'

The chief made his decision and the warriors cheered him for it. Chip made a final desperate plea. 'Let your young squaws and children come with me, then. Or don't you want to see this tribe continue?'

Chip's offer made sense to the chief. There was no need for the womenfolk and children to die under the army's shells and sabres. The chief roared out his orders and the squaws, young and old, slim and fat, carrying babies or ushering them ahead of them, flooded the narrow avenues. It was a raggle-taggle procession, the older women babbling in protest at leaving their menfolk. Chip sighed irritably. The cavalry were advancing, too close for comfort, and it was only the river that halted their progress. He nodded curtly at Sam. 'Take them down and show them where they can shelter. I'll ride on and see if I can talk peace with the cavalry major.'

'Some hope,' muttered Sam. 'He's a murderous beast.'

Sam drove the procession of evacuees out of the settlement. Chip urged his horse into a gallop, heading for the biggest shock of his life.

10

Sam arrived at Chip's spread ushering
the procession of Crow women and
their bewildered children ahead of
him. Many of the spirited, young
squaws remained mutinous over
deserting their homely tepees and
were suspicious when they entered the
comfortable farmhouse. The large
rooms with thick rugs on the floor
and silk-covered furniture were foreign
to them, while the bedrooms with
beds high off the floor seemed
unnatural.

For the moment, Sam was at a loss
how to deal with them, but Gentle
Sunrise, who had been watching both
the advance of the cavalry and the
advance of the Crow people took
charge of the situation in her usual
blunt fashion. She led them to the big
barn where they were more cheerful

and at home among the straw mattresses and the two Indian boys were there to look after them.

Back in the farmhouse, Dee was up and about, showing a willingness to play her part in the drama that was inevitable. She peered through the window at the front of the big house and watched Chip confront the major commanding the column of troops. The army man looked angry and Dee shut her eyes and muttered a quick prayer that no harm should come to Chip.

★   ★   ★

Major Rod Ross reined in his horse and raised his gloved hand as a signal for the column to halt. He glared at the horseman blocking his path, then frowned heavily in utter surprise, recognizing the features that at this moment were a mixture of astonishment and hostility.

'Hell's bells! My horse-trading brother. It must be ten years at least?'

'Still the bully-boy, eh?'

'You need a bit of grit for this job, Chip.'

'Killing Indians? Is that a job?'

'Ridding the land of savage heathens. I find it satisfactory.'

'The most savage tribes and the white man can live together if they respect each other.'

'Oh, I heard in Hometown,' boomed Rod, 'what an Indian lover you are.'

'I trade with the Crow.'

'They are squatting on land wanted by the railways.'

'And if they make a stand?'

'I have my orders. We will wipe out the whole tribe.'

'Kill them, just to fill Hoot Clackson's pockets with railway dollars?'

'I am not interested in civilians' dealings. I'm an army man, proud of it and this is an operation I'm bound to carry out.'

'And you are on my land. I own it as far as the river. You are trespassing.'

'I have to cross your land to reach the

196

Crow settlement.'

'Not without my permission, Brother.'

'The Army goes where it likes. Now, stand aside and let us through.'

'Turn back, Rod. We don't want to see a war. Tell your masters to talk peace.'

'Wake up, Chip. You are holding up progress. When the railway comes, and it will spread all over the territory, the day of the horse will finish.'

'And me with it I suppose?'

'I guess so.'

'How do you figure that, Brother?'

'No more cattle-drives. The cowboy will vanish when the cattle will go to the markets by rail. You will be wise to sell up now, Chip, while your stock gets good prices.'

'And will the coming of the railway mean the end of the cavalry?' asked Chip evenly.

Major Rod Ross's face darkened. 'Always the one with the smart wisecrack, weren't you?'

'I'm just pointing out there will be a

need for horses, even when the railways run east and west across this vast territory.'

The major turned in his saddle. His troops were growing restless. He'd trained them to fever pitch and they were raring to have a go at the Indians. Even the horses were snorting and fidgeting. He scowled at his brother's iron-hard features, the cold glint in his eyes, and thought it sad there was no display of affection between them. No semblance of a smile or brotherly love. In fact Chip was an obstacle who had to be removed and because his attitude towards the Indians was completely opposite to that of the major's he was prepared to use force to carry out his orders. 'We've wasted too much time talking. Move aside, Chip.'

'Would you shoot your own flesh and blood?'

The major realized the eyes of all his men were upon him. They knew him as a hard, ruthless officer, who never backed down or retreated in the face of danger. He'd reached a crisis point. His brother had challenged him to put duty above sentiment, but the major fell short of killing his own brother. Instead he raised his riding whip and brought it down upon Chip's shoulder with such a brutal force it tore apart his shirt and left an angry streak of blood across his flesh. Chip staggered back and impulsively went for his guns. His brother, alarmed at Chip's reaction, struck with the whip again to prevent any gunplay. The whip curled round Chip's hands burning them savagely and he could not feel them to draw his guns. A third strike with the whip lashed Chip's legs, sending him off-balance and he collapsed to the ground, sending up a cloud of dust. Rod scowled at his brother, helpless beneath him, legs kicking the air and flat on his back.

'Stay out of my business in future.'

Chip glared back at him. Humiliated, more than sore from the blows, he muttered, 'I'll not forget this, Brother.'

The major yelled an order to his troops. 'Forward! Prepare to charge!'

Chip watched the procession rattle past. Horses broke into a gallop. Riders drew sabres. Wagons and field guns bounced across the uneven ground and then the whole column launched itself into the river, crossing the shallow water and hauling itself on to the opposite bank. The momentum barely subsided and the enthusiastic major led his men forward with a joy that sickened Chip.

Now, the force was within sight of the Crow tepees. The cavalry whooped fanatically and charged towards the narrow avenues between the tepees. The Crow warriors were out of sight, taking up positions in the tepees and flighting their deadly arrows through the slight gaps between the flaps at the front of the tepees. The cavalry met a hail of missiles. Arrows, spears and tomahawks. The horses could only advance in single file. The Crow warriors leapt upon the individual riders, using knives and stone-headed clubs. Hand-to-hand fighting took its toll. The troopers fired pistols at point-blank range and cut down their attackers with their swinging sabres. But Major Ross didn't expect such resistance. He reached the end of the camp unscathed. He paused to look back. He saw in his wake as many casualties among his men as had been inflicted upon the Indian tribe. Wounded horses writhed on the ground in agony and the amount of carnage in such a short stretch of battlefield astonished him.

The Crow defensive formation with its narrow, confined tracks between the tepees had cleverly restricted the cavalry's movements and the major had fallen foul of it through his own crazy tactics. The charge he'd led was the arrogant attack by a troop of superior trained men with superior weapons and the major had discarded caution. Now, he faced the humiliation of ordering his force to withdraw. He rode out of the settlement, followed by his swearing, frustrated troopers to reform, count the cost of the futile attack and plan fresh tactics. 'What's the tally, Sergeant-Major Robins?' he demanded.

'Twenty troopers killed, fifteen wounded. And we've lost thirty horses.' There was deep resentment in the man's voice and Ross could barely face the dejected survivors of that first battle. His eyes were heavy with guilt and his face twitched nervously. He'd wanted to win medals by wiping out the savage heathens, but after this catastrophe, he would be bound to explain the loss of so many men to his superior officers in Washington, and he would be lucky if a court-martial did not follow.

He was convinced his men no longer trusted his leadership. He'd been too wild, allowing his hatred for the Indians to cloud his judgement, and wasn't there a certain amount of contempt for his brother that urged him to make short work of the Crow tribe?

He remained on his horse and was forced to witness the depressing sight of the medical officer and his team of orderlies bringing in the dead and wounded on the back of a wagon. He realized he had to do something dramatic to win back the confidence of his men. The sixty-five survivors of the first attack looked mutinous as they sprawled shaken on the ground and the major doubted if they would respond to any of his orders. He knew his only way to lift morale was to gain victory over the Crow tribe, destroy them and their settlement completely. 'Bring forward the guns,' he shouted to the gunners.

The field guns were trundled into the open. The gunnery officer ordered them to be stripped for action. Shells were piled behind the guns. The major's troopers stirred from their sombre mood and looked on in interest, as if this was meant to be an entertainment for their benefit.

The field guns were brought to bear on the distant tepees. The Crow settlement was within range. Major Ross narrowed his eyes and there was a cruel smile on his white face. 'Blast them to hell!' he shouted.

The shells whined across the clear sky and then dropped among the tepees. Rocks and soil flew upwards as deep shell craters were carved out of the ground. Tepees caught fire and horrific screams echoed from within. The settlement became blackened with smoke and the acrid smell of cordite drifted over the territory. It took thirty minutes for the settlement to be reduced to ashes. The tepees smouldered and collapsed. Major Ross smiled hugely. His troops climbed to their feet and cheered. The gunners ceased fire, let the guns cool and then cleaned them. The major ordered tents to be pitched close to the river bank, the camp now in no-man's land. He posted sentries, although he felt confident there were no Indians alive to counter-attack. Hot meals were issued and the troops rested, feeling they had won a famous victory.

★   ★   ★

Across the river, sheltering in Chip's barn, the Crow womenfolk were frantic with despair. They had watched from the high loft of the barn as the shells had rained mercilessly on their menfolk, defending the Crow settlement and seen the black smoke as the tepees had burned to the ground.

The women shivered and wailed, they were isolated and mourned the loss of their warrior male, who hunted and provided meat for them and their children. The shrill, uninhibited cries swept into the army lines and angered the troops as they lay in their tents.

★　★　★

Chip had seen the Crow settlement destroyed as he stood at the window of the large bedroom. His face was pale with fury. 'My God! I never thought it would come to this. Field guns against bows and arrows.'

Gentle Sunrise trembled with remorse, her fingers grappling with the buckskin cape she was draping over her shoulders. She picked up her large medicine bag. 'I must return to the settlement. A few of my people may still be alive, but badly hurt.'

Chip looked alarmed. 'You daren't go through the army lines.'

'I have to. How else will I reach the settlement?'

Sam Cotter gave her a solemn nod. 'I'll escort you,' he said and patted his gun holsters.

Dee, still pale, but now a very determined woman, volunteered to go along with them. Her voice was husky and she was weak from the days she had spent sick and helpless, but she felt she owed Gentle Sunrise something for saving her life. 'If I can be of any help as a nurse?' she suggested.

'Don't be foolish,' rapped Chip. 'You have only just got out of a sick bed.'

He put out objections as to why they shouldn't venture through the army lines and Sam thought it was unlike him. Chip was always prepared to take risks if it meant helping his Indian friends, and he could only conclude that Chip was weighed down with guilt over his brother's inhuman act in turning the field guns on to the Crow settlement.

'We will go,' decided Gentle Sunrise.

'Wait!'

Chip regarded the trio, knowing what they were determined to do was right. He sensed there was a danger of another conflict with his brother and he feared the outcome. He was filled with shame because of the major's sadistic destruction of the Crow settlement and he realized if his brother showed pride for what he'd achieved, Chip might be tempted to draw his guns on his own flesh and blood. 'You'll need me to get you past the army sentries. We'll take a wagon.'

Sam helped him to harness a pair of mules to a hay-wagon and they put a canvas tilt over it to shelter any casualties from the fierce sunlight that ravaged the open land. Chip drove the wagon towards the river. The mules strained to haul it up the bank and then plunged into the shallow water. It had not rained for several weeks and at the distant end of the river the waterfall splashed lazily over the rugged formation of moss-covered granite boulders.

Ahead of them, the white tents of the army lines lay still, the slow-moving figures of the sentries with rifles strapped to their shoulders, patrolled the perimeter of the camp. They looked weary and complacent as if the job they had been sent to do was finished and guard duties were just a whim of an eccentric commander, who had to keep up the appearance of the strict army disciplinarian no matter what the situation was. A man coughed twice and then sneezed and he sounded loud enough and distressed to awaken the whole camp. Chip drove straight for the army lines, the grating of the wagon wheels and the plodding hoofs of the mules, together with the jangling of the harness, caused the pair of sentries slouching to and fro between the tents to pause and stare at the wagon with more curiosity than alertness. Chip pulled on the reins and halted the mules.

One of the sentries, tall and thin, his uniform dirty and shabby, pulled his rifle from his shoulder and held it menacingly in front of him. His eyes watered and his nose was like a ripe plum. His face was pouring sweat and his complexion looked as if it was on fire. He breathed painfully in short gasps. 'Where do you think you're going?' he asked Chip surlily.

His words were punctuated with coughs and sneezes, the cough racking his body till it almost knocked him off his feet. Gentle Sunrise frowned down at the sentry from the front of the wagon. 'You are a sick man. Why aren't you in bed?'

'Fat chance o' that when I've just come on duty. Four miserable hours to see through yet.'

'You look as if you've caught a flu bug, Soldier.'

'So has half the population in Hometown. Reckon we brought it with us, 'cause it's spreading through the camp like a fire.'

Chip stared mystified at the young Indian medicine girl. She'd just seen the slaughter of her warriors by these soldiers and here she was showing concern over one of them as if he was her patient. She must have a heart of gold. Chip was blessed with little compassion for the sick soldier and he said bluntly, 'I want to talk to Major Ross.'

'The major is resting.'

'He'll talk to me.'

The sentry wasn't impressed by Chip's claim. The wagon carried a motley collection and they had no right to penetrate the army lines. He narrowed his eyes suspiciously at Chip. 'Why should he talk to you?'

'I happen to be his brother.'

The sentry was overcome with a fresh

spasm of coughing and sneezing and Gentle Sunrise winced at the soldier's condition. When he'd recovered he signalled to his colleague to go and fetch the major.

Rod Ross stamped out of his tent in a foul mood. Half-dressed, he hadn't forgotten the unpleasant encounter he'd had with Chip earlier, but he was too inquisitive to ignore his brother and wondered what he was doing loitering in the camp perimeter. He scowled up at Chip, who sat holding the reins of the mules. 'This'd better be important.'

'Will you let us through?'

'Why? Where are you heading?'

'To the Crow settlement.'

'For what reason?'

'There may be wounded there who need help.'

'Forget it, Chip. My gunners did a great job. Nothing in that camp has survived.'

'We must make sure.'

'What if there is some heathen savage

feeling sorry for himself? What can you do for him?'

Gentle Sunrise had sat and listened to the major's cruel dialogue with a furious temper swelling up inside her. The delay was frustrating enough, but to hear her people called heathen savages made her snap. She pushed forward, glowering down at the major, wild-eyed and full of contempt.

'How can this evil man be your brother, Chip? He's the very devil himself!'

Rod Ross took exception at being called the devil by an Indian squaw. His square jaw quivered and his lips closed into a thin, sulky line.

'Who are you calling a devil, squaw?'

'You! A heartless beast, that you are.'

Chip had wanted to be diplomatic, even slightly patronizing towards his brother to gain permission to pass through the army lines, but it appeared the Crow medicine girl's hot temper had ruined his approach.

The major sneered at the Indian girl,

his mouth a cynical expression displaying his indifference to her passionate opinion. 'How is it you did not perish along with your heathen brothers?'

She wasn't given the chance to reply. Dee burst forth from the folds of the wagon's canvas tilt, trembling with agitation after listening to the major's careless consideration of the Crow people. Rod stared at the beautiful Dee and was taken aback as to why such a delicate creature was involved in this mission. She simply didn't fit in with the rest. The major resorted to his famous northern charm and good manners and bowed politely to the stage star. 'I'm sorry, ma'am. I fear I haven't been introduced.'

'That doesn't matter,' stormed Dee. 'This squaw was busy saving my life while your troops carried out the atrocities on her people.'

Her lithe body shook with anger as she accused the major. Rod's eyebrows shot up and his cheeks were inflamed as the word atrocities stung his ears.

Atrocities were the savage deeds carried out by the Indian tribes on the white settlers and when they ambushed army patrols. The United States Cavalry did not stoop to such inhuman tactics. His square jaw dropped as he regarded Dee, his breathing was heavy and he tried his hardest not to look hostile. Like most military men, vain in their smart uniforms, he had a sharp eye for a lovely woman and while he'd hoped to make an impression upon Dee he felt she'd insulted him. He came back at her, determined to show how important a man he was. 'I have been given the job of clearing this territory and occupying it till the railway people take over. They are my orders. The Crow tribe preferred to stay and fight my men, so what else could we do but wipe them out?'

'You haven't wiped us out,' cried Gentle Sunrise, impulsively.

Chip knew it was a mistake for the Indian medicine girl to speak out of turn. His brother smirked at the girl and said absently, 'Oh, I know about the Crow women and children sheltering in Chip's barn. The next generation of the tribe, eh! I cannot allow them to remain.'

'What do you intend to do, turn the field guns on them?' demanded Chip.

Hard man that he was, Rod was beginning to feel the shame of his outrageous tactics in defeating the Crow warriors and any reminder of it undermined his authority.

'I want them out of here.'

'They will stay all the while I'm on my land,' argued Chip.

'That can only be till the railway people buy you out. I know for a fact a party of them are travelling by coach to Hometown to settle all the details.'

'I'm not budging unless they meet my price.'

'You really are asking for brother to fight brother, aren't you? I'm giving you fair warning, Chip, get rid of those savages.'

'What do you mean? Get rid of them?'

215

Rod shrugged. 'Take them to the distant hills, well out of the way of this land.'

'The hills are barren. Useless for farming and the wild animals have deserted them for better pastures. In the winter, nothing survives up there.'

'Then take them with you when you have to move out. You'll be heading further west, I reckon.'

'I'm going nowhere till I meet these railway barons.'

Rod half-turned on his heel. The permission to pass through his lines unresolved. He glanced back at the indignant faces hating him from the wagon, and then to demonstrate what a powerful man he was, especially for the benefit of Dee, he said, with a swagger, 'You, may visit the Crow settlement and find what you will.'

Chip eyed him suspiciously. 'Why the sudden change of heart?'

'A deal, brother. I'll give you till sunrise.'

The major pointed a finger straight at

Chip's distant barn. 'If those Crow savages aren't out of there, I'll see to it my troops chase them far and wide.'

He said no more, but the party in the wagon could imagine what would happen if the troops were set upon the helpless woman and children sheltering in Chip's barn. It would only be a chase till they were caught and put to the sword. The major stalked back to his tent and the sentries stood aside to allow Chip to drive the wagon towards the destroyed Crow settlement. Chip gave his young partner Sam Cotter an anxious look. There was just the two of them and two women against a troop of cavalry. Sam bit his lips and fidgeted awkwardly. He'd been left out of the recent conversation because he failed to understand how two brothers could be so different. One willing to make friends with the Indians, the other persecuting them at every opportunity. 'Reckon we got a lot to do before sunrise, Chip,' he said ruefully.

Chip stared in the distance, across

the broad river at his spread. He suddenly felt cold at leaving the place unprotected, but he couldn't be in two places at once. 'I don't trust my brother,' he said.

'Surely, he won't go against his word. He is a man of honour, isn't he?' queried Sam.

'The Sioux slaughtered my parents and sisters in a wagon train raid when Rod and me were out hunting. Rod's had no honour since where Indians are concerned. He's spent ten years on a revenge mission and he's still not satisfied.'

The wagon rolled into the blackened Crow settlement. The sickening smell caused all of the wagon occupants to cover their noses. 'What an awful stench!' protested Dee.

'The smell of death,' said Chip grimly.

11

Chip and Sam forged ahead to meet the worst of the carnage, hoping to forestall the womenfolk in what was bound to be a distressing sight. Gentle Sunrise would not be thwarted, however. She was a medicine woman and her duty lay in the forefront of any disaster. She sprang off the wagon clutching her medicine bag to her, and Dee, insistent on helping followed her.

'There don't seem much anyone can do,' decided Chip, 'except take these poor wretches to their burial ground.'

Sam's face was distorted as if in pain. It was unbelievable what bedlam the field guns had caused. Craters in the ground made it dangerous to search the area. They were deep and dark and to fall into one could result in a broken limb. The tepees were in ashes and the well-directed shells had made certain the occupants perished when the tepees caught fire.

'Don't give up hope,' pleaded Gentle Sunrise.

Her lovely features were set like stone and she shivered with pent-up emotion as the two men raked over the debris. Dee had turned quite green, never having come across such a ghastly scene in all of her previously sheltered life, but she was determined to stick it out. She'd thrown in her lot with the rugged Chip and was committed to share the rough with the smooth whatever his future might hold. She shook off the distasteful nausea and, when Chip turned on her quite brusquely, telling her to return to the wagon, she rebelled strongly. 'I'm hating every second of this, but for the first time in my life I can understand why the redskins hate the white man. I shall remember this experience till I die and it won't do me any harm.'

'Stop talking! Listen!' warned Sam.

The silence that followed was eerie,

the four of them standing perfectly still in the macabre surroundings, not speaking, but straining their ears.

'I hear nothing,' said Gentle Sunrise, biting her lips.

She longed for at least one survivor and if Sam had heard anything that would make their mission worthwhile the painful silence that followed depressed her.

'What did you hear, Sam?' asked Chip.

'A low moan.'

'Jackals, I'll wager. They can smell death a mile away.'

'No, Chip! There it is again.'

The low moan broke the silence. It was pitiful and pleading. Gentle Sunrise waited no longer. She charged forward, ankle-deep in black debris, chasing the mournful sound. The others followed. Nobody felt cheerful at what they might find.

The medicine woman had detected from where the sound came and beyond one of the charred tepees a young warrior lay apparently lifeless on the ground. Gentle Sunrise flung herself beside him, examining his wounds and ripping open her medicine bag. Chip pulled up suddenly and grabbed Sam by the arm. 'There must be something here that hasn't burned to the ground. We'll make a stretcher to carry him to the wagon.'

A despairing screech from Gentle Sunrise drove out her pent-up emotion. She dropped her clinical approach and sat on her knees, hands to her head, tears flooding her gentle face as she recoiled in horror. The warrior's wildly staring eyes flickered as the Crow girl's shrill voice echoed through the moonlit night. They had been hours searching, hoping for at least one survivor, but it now seemed Gentle Sunrise hated what she'd discovered. 'Oh! It's Silent Hunter!'

Chip and Sam ran back to where the Crow girl sat stunned next to her patient. Chip wondered if the young warrior could call himself lucky. It was obvious Silent Hunter had been blown clear of his tepee by shell-blast and escaped the flames that had seen his brothers perish. But on closer examination, the shrapnel that had scattered when the shell exploded had peppered the Crow warrior's legs. Deep gashes holed his flesh and he'd lost a vast amount of blood. He remained tight-lipped as Gentle Sunrise looked into his pain-filled eyes as if he was ashamed of making a fuss about his wounds and, although he fought bravely against the cruel pain, it was sapping his strength. Gentle Sunrise saw him weakening and quickly pulled herself together after the shock of recognizing the sole survivor.

She turned upon Chip and Sam, who for the moment were idle and said crossly, 'I thought you two were going to rig up a stretcher?'

Embarrassed, the two men stalked off to search for wooden poles and remnants of animals' skins, while Dee was sent sprinting to the wagon to fetch a canvas container of fresh water. The

Crow medicine woman spent twenty minutes stopping the flow of blood and heavily bandaging the warrior's legs. It was impossible for him to walk now, and doubtful if he'd ever walk with that graceful, athletic stride that made him such a striking young man. The wounded warrior sipped water and recovered slightly from the traumatic ordeal he'd suffered. He did not speak, which worried Gentle Sunrise, and in his frozen features there was an expression of savage hostility. Chip and Sam managed to prepare a makeshift stretcher and carried the warrior to the wagon. The moon sailed towards the skyline and the darkness reminded Chip of the deadline he was forced to meet at his brother's demand. A return to his own lines by daybreak or the troopers would be set upon the women and children sheltering in the big barn. Because of the sorely wounded Silent Hunter the wagon had to be driven gingerly over the rough surface and progress towards Chip's spread was irritatingly slow.

The sentries patrolling the camp perimeter of the army lines signalled the wagon through and when the party was home and dry, Sam unhitched the mules from the wagon, the wounded Silent Hunter was given a comfortable bed on the ground floor of Chip's house. To preserve his peace and quiet he was left on his own in a small front room, and Gentle Sunrise, after changing his dressings on arrival, spent the night cat-napping in an adjoining room.

The young warrior had not yet uttered a word and Gentle Sunrise feared he was suffering from more than physical injuries, but when he finally slipped into an exhausted sleep, breathing normally, the Crow medicine woman was able to relax.

With the whole house now quiet, Silent Hunter stirred. His legs were afire and the perspiration bathed his face and body. He raised himself and looked across the small room, which Chip used as his office. On the desk there was a tray with a bottle of whisky and two glasses. Chip was only a modest drinker, but kept some liquor in the house to entertain the horse dealers who came to bargain with him.

Silent Hunter had never tasted the 'firewater' which his elders claimed cured all ills and sorrows and put new life into tired bodies, and his gaze became riveted on the bottle of amber liquid till the temptation grew too much for him. He was convinced the 'firewater' was the answer to the bold plan he had in mind, although to reach the desk would be an ordeal in itself.

The pain of simply moving his stiff and aching body was something he could ignore, but he knew his legs were useless and he was weak from the loss of blood. It was quite a struggle to shift the single, heavy blanket off of his lean body, and he lay in the bed panting for a few minutes. He regained his breath and it felt quite pleasant just to lie there resting, but he had this incredible determination, that to most men in his condition was beyond belief, to carry out a mission of revenge.

He slid to the floor without making a sound then turned on all fours and attempted to crawl across the room, but there was no power in his legs to drive him forward and he collapsed on his face. He gritted his teeth, angry and frustrated with his fragile condition; he used his elbows as his main force of energy and slithered from the bed to the desk. Despite his long arms, reaching the bottle from his prone position was an exhausting exercise. Finally, his fingers closed round the bottle and he dragged it down where it fell in his lap. A wild excitement invaded his weary eyes as he held up the bottle, three-quarters full of the liquor. He pulled the cork with his teeth and the fumes struck him, pungent and bitter. He turned his head away and his throat was filled with nausea, but he realized his elders couldn't be wrong about the 'firewater'. It must taste better than it smelt and the effect was tremendous, like good medicine.

He took a long gulp and the perspiration on his face gleamed. When he lowered the bottle to draw a second breath his whole body glowed and it was true what he'd heard; it filled him with energy and lifted his spirits till he was convinced there was nothing he couldn't do, regardless of his disablement.

His second mouthful of the liquor went straight to his head and despite the dizzy feeling, his boldness bordered on the jaunty. He remembered to check upon his long, hunting knife dangling from his buckskin tunic and then fortified by the whisky he slithered to the door of the room.

His movements were slow and silent, but after he'd opened the door and wriggled along the passage there was only the front door of the house to negotiate to escape. The liquor had numbed his senses to such an extent that he found he was able to kneel without his legs giving way under him.

He unlatched the stout timber door

and dragged himself out into the open. The moon was half-hidden by cloud and a shaft of orange light swept across the cobbled yard, struck the outbuildings and paved a narrow track into the rows of white tents where the cavalry troop were under canvas.

He pulled the hunting knife from his waistband and gripped it in his teeth in case he needed the weapon for instant use then headed for the Army lines.

The night air struck him and his head spun. The dizzy spell affected his vision and the way ahead was blurred. He had never known what it was like to be drunk and he blamed his wounds for the erratic, zig-zag course he followed. He swam into the thick grass that lay before the river bank and the dew was cooling and refreshed him. He hauled himself up on the bank and slipped into the water and found it easier to float across to the opposite bank on his back than to employ his natural free-style of swimming.

He rested to regain his breath, his

eyes scanning the camp. Hacking coughs from the tents echoed towards him and he observed that there were only a pair of sentries patrolling the entire area. He watched them amble to and fro and when they reached the end of their patch it left him with a hundred yards of open space. He slithered unseen towards the tents, looked up and saw the one he wanted. The commanding officer's pennant flew from a mast outside. Silent Hunter knew that the hardest part of his mission was accomplished. He crept forward and untied the cords that secured the flaps of the tent and sneaked inside. The major lay on top of his camp bed, half-dressed without his tunic or boots. Silent Hunter advanced, but the tension made him excited and the whisky he'd consumed on an empty stomach caused him to belch loudly. The major, who was never more than half-asleep when he retired for the night, bolted upright and snatched the pistol he kept loaded on the small bedside table. 'Who is there!' he bellowed.

Silent Hunter lay flat on the ground, aware that he was a difficult target, and while the major scanned the interior of his tent among the flitting shadows, the Crow warrior plucked the hunting knife from his mouth and with one aim threw the knife by the tip of the blade at the victim, sitting upright on the bed. The knife darted towards the major, twisting, and struck, the thick blade thrusting straight into his heart. He uttered a short cry of pain, rolled off the bed and scattered the small table with all of its contents. The noise travelled along the row of tents. The troopers were alerted and rushed out into the open, undressed but brandishing what weapons they picked up at the sound of the commotion. The sentries on duty raced to the major's tent, bayonets fixed to their rifles. Silent Hunter sneaked out of the tent. His mission of revenge was completed and the honour of his tribe maintained. He was totally exhausted and the pain in his legs crippled his simplest movements. The escape from the army camp to return to his friends seemed an insurmountable task, but it didn't seem to matter.

For a while, he lay low while the soldiers ran around in circles, and he felt satisfied when he heard the shout relayed through the lines, 'The major has been murdered!'

The soldiers were called out in strength to mount a manhunt. Lanterns were brought and, led by a young, determined lieutenant, the area was combed and the perimeter cordoned off by extra guards.

Silent Hunter realized it would soon be daybreak and his presence would be immediately discovered. If he was to make a desperate effort to escape he must make his move now. He crept away from the shadow of the tents and slowly inched his way towards the perimeter of the camp, but the soldiers were swinging their lanterns so that the light was shining at ground level. He wriggled out into the open and attempted to drag himself to the river. A shaft of light fell on him, revealing him like a spotlight on a stage.

'There he is!' shouted a sentry.

A score of troops ran towards the Crow warrior and without any thought of arresting him, they fired a volley of shots into his body, and threw his corpse into the river.

It did not end there. Although the troopers owed no special loyalty or affection towards the major, often he drove them to the point of mutiny, they could not bear the humiliation of an Indian breaking into the camp to kill him.

There were hotheads among the depleted ranks of the troops who actually enjoyed killing Indians and suddenly they ran amok. Discipline was ignored and despite the young lieuten-ant ordering them back to their tents, thirty angry soldiers, led by a veteran, grizzled sergeant, marched out of camp, crossed the river and headed for Chip's spread. The lieutenant was reduced to a helpless witness. He was watching the remnants of the whole force acting crazily. Out of the seventy men who'd survived the disastrous cavalry charge on the Crow settlement, forty of them had gone down with the flu epidemic and most of them were in a bad way. The medical officer and his three orderlies were working round the clock without much success.

★   ★   ★

Gentle Sunrise was the first to break into the adjoining room, where she'd left Silent Hunter to recover, when the volley of shots echoed from the army camp. She was petrified to find him missing and raised the alarm, which brought Chip, Sam and the Indian houseboys, together with a sleepy-eyed Dee crowding into the room.

They had not been there long enough to consider what action to take when the reflection from the lanterns the advancing mob were carrying bounced off the front windows of the house.

It looked a raggle-taggle procession. The troops were only half-dressed, but heavily armed with sabres and rifles, shouting obscene oaths as they headed for the big barn.

Gentle Sunrise stared in dismay at Chip. 'There are a hundred Crow women and children in there. Surely . . . '

'I've got a feeling Silent Hunter has put the fox among the hens,' Chip said ruefully.

'We must stop them!' cried the Crow medicine woman.

Sam gave Chip a questioning glance. 'Reckon you have to take sides now, Chip. Either we protect the Crow families or you simply let these troops slaughter the lot of them.'

Chip turned on the young man, red faced with indignation. 'If you think I'm taking up arms against my fellow men you are mistaken. I've been the go-between to keep peace in this territory and it has worked without a show of strength.'

Sam nodded curtly at the advancing soldiers. As they drew closer to the barn their rowdiness and anger was frightening, and they were in no mood to listen to reason. 'Are you going out there to talk peace to that mob?'

Chip strode to the door. He'd buckled his gunbelt to his waist when he'd first heard the volley of shots explode from the army lines, now he removed it and dropped the belt and his pair of guns on a chair.

'That's what I'm figuring on doing.'

'Unarmed! Chip, you're mad!'

Dee rushed into his arms and stared pleadingly into his eyes. 'You daren't do it. That mob will cut you down before you can open your mouth.'

She clung to him so fiercely he was unable to move. Sam had seen the worst side of the army cavalry that day and he had no hesitation in taking action to defend the helpless women and children sheltering in the barn. In the room there was a glass-fronted cabinet that contained six rifles. Sam crossed over to it and came back with an armful of guns and boxes of shells. He dished out the rifles. 'Anyone who don't know how to handle a rifle, I'll teach you.'

The Indian houseboys looked confused as they nursed the guns and Gentle Sunrise accepted that guns were taboo in the redskins' hands. Chip was livid with Sam's reckless behaviour. 'What the devil do you think you are doing?'

'I'm going to talk to that mob in the only language they know.'

He was out of the door before Chip could restrain him and came face to face with the veteran sergeant who was a few yards out in front of his men.

Despite Sam being outnumbered by thirty-to-one the soldiers shuffled to a halt. The crude oaths faded and the sergeant squinted at Sam. 'You figuring on using that rifle, kid?'

'Maybe. What is it you want?'

'We're after revenge.'

'For what?'

'One of them heathen savages has murdered the major!'

The sergeant shouted his reply and the startling news reached the ears of Chip as he positioned himself in the open doorway. There was little love lost between him and his Indian-hating brother, especially after the major had turned the field guns on to the Crow settlement and demolished it.

They were flesh and blood, however, and Rod Ross had been killed by a Crow warrior, whom Chip had befriended. Chip frowned at Gentle Sunrise, standing at his shoulder. 'Silent Hunter has killed my brother. Why couldn't he leave things as they were? There has been more than enough bloodshed.'

'Did you expect a Crow warrior not to seek revenge?'

Chip stared straight ahead of him at the restless soldiers. 'And this mob want a wholesale slaughter to avenge their major.'

He went forward and the rest of his party followed. The six of them lined up, with Sam in the centre, all holding rifles at the ready. The veteran sergeant's eyes bulged. 'You lot must be bluffing.'

'No, we just want to talk sense,' said Chip.

'What if me and my boys ain't likely to listen?'

'If there's to be any shooting, Sergeant, a lot of you will go with us,' retorted Chip.

The sergeant licked his lips and found himself staring down the rifle barrel held by Dee. 'You'd put a beautiful woman in the firing line to fight your battles? That ain't right, mister.'

'I'm here because I want to be,' snapped Dee.

'My brother's been killed and your soldiers have made the Crow warrior pay for it. Let the matter end there, eh?'

'Your brother!' frowned the sergeant.

'Major Rod Ross was my brother.'

'Then you have good reason to get shot of the Crow tribe you have given shelter to. Damn it, man. You should be on our side,' insisted the sergeant.

'I don't take sides, but if this tit-for-tat doesn't soon end how can there be peace between the Indians and the white man?' said Chip.

'How can your Indian friends show us peace?' sneered the sergeant.

'I can,' volunteered Gentle Sunrise.

The sergeant narrowed his eyes meanly at the medicine woman. 'You!'

Gentle Sunrise had felt the death of Silent Hunter keenly. The young warrior was of the true blood of his forefathers, brave and impulsive, a savage fighter who had died without regrets. For the sake of peace and the protection of the Crow women and children, she was willing to devalue her standing in the tribe. 'There are many soldiers very ill with the flu epidemic and your medical officer must be finding it impossible to cope alone. I can treat your men with willow bark which will take away the pain and bring down the fever.'

'Flaming witchcraft! Hocus-pocus. Don't give me the screamers with your medicine, squaw!'

'Gentle Sunrise saved my life,' Dee lashed at him.

The arrogant sergeant was silenced instantly. Behind him his men had gradually lost the appetite for more fighting, especially as they had to get past six rifles pointing at them. Some of them too, were feeling unwell in the chilly night air. The sergeant realized there was only one inexperienced, young lieutenant to run the troop, now the major was dead, and they had to occupy a lot of territory till the railway people arrived to take over. If many more soldiers went sick he'd be hard put to post enough sentries to guard the widespread acres.

He shrugged and said, 'All right, let's put the guns away and call a truce. The medicine woman can treat the flu victims. The Crow women and children will be safe.'

'I'll fetch my bag,' said Gentle Sunrise.

'And I'll come with you,' said Dee.

12

Now the dangerous crisis had been replaced by a truce, it was remarkable how the soldiers and the Crow tribe worked together. Gentle Sunrise and Dee worked tirelessly together with the army medical officer to give comfort to the flu victims. Those soldiers still on their feet went with Crow teenage boys to the waterfall to collect the fresh spring water and cut slices of the white willow bark to treat the sick.

The women and children, who'd been shut up in the barn for their own safety, now were free to roam the territory and enjoy the good, fresh air without fear of reprisals. The children played and found a shy rapport with those soldiers, who lounged in the sun recovering from the flu, while the womenfolk sat in bunches, knitting with their porcupine needles.

'This is how it ought to be,' said Chip, gazing on the peaceful scene from the porchway of his house.

The sun reflected on the slow-moving river and the waterfall looked like diamonds cascading from the cluster of rocks above.

'If the railway people drive you out you'll miss this place,' ventured Sam.

'I bought this spread dirt cheap and I've done well out of it. They'll have to bargain hard to get this land. Maybe, they've got the Crow acres for nothing and that scoundrel Hoot Clackson is willing to sell out without making a stand, but unless they meet my terms, the railway won't be able to run because my land is plumb in the middle.'

'Where will you head for if you lose Camp Waterfall?'

'Anywhere that's good for raising and selling horses. I fancy California, but to be honest I'd rather stay where I am. Dee's pitching her lot in with me, and I'd like you as a partner, Sam.'

'You won't have to ask me twice.'

'I dunno what's to become of the Crow women and children, though. Silent Hunter would have made a good chief. They must have land to settle.'

For the moment, the Crow tribe had been given peace while under Chip's protection, but when the railway people took over the old Crow settlement the Indians would be forced into a nomadic existence without any menfolk to look after them.

Chip spotted the Morgan and the Quarter Horse cantering in the corral, the pair of animals belonging to Anvil Smith in Hometown he'd hired out to Sam and Dee.

'While things have quietened down here, Sam, I reckon it'll be a good time to return those horses.'

Sam nodded reflectively. 'Seems years ago since Silent Hunter stole that Morgan.'

'And when he saved our lives,' added Chip.

'He proved to be a good friend. What he did . . . '

'In his mind it had to be done, even if Rod Ross was my brother.'

'Water under the bridge now.'

'Nothing to be gained by harping on about it, Sam. You'd best get going. Hometown's a three-day journey. Maybe a couple of the troopers will escort you.'

'Chip, I ain't no greenhorn! I can take care of myself.'

'And I ain't forgetting that wretch of an ex-sheriff and his posse of outlaws are still at large.'

Sam scratched the light stubble of his boyish chin. 'I'd forgotten about Sully,' he admitted.

Sam was able to enlist two troopers, who hadn't fallen foul of the flu epidemic and were glad of the opportunity to get away from the camp. Sam saddled Taffy, the mustang he'd captured and broken-in and the small procession of three men and five horses set off.

The trail to Hometown was thick with dust and hadn't been used since the cavalry regiment had descended upon Camp Waterfall, and for the three days it took Sam and his escort to reach the town, it was simply a routine of riding, resting, cooking meals and sleeping in the open. Things were different in Hometown. It was still the lawless town Sam remembered before he moved on to Chip's spread. Heavy boozing and gambling went on all day, which inevitably resulted in furious brawls and, as there was no lawman to keep the peace, guns were no longer confiscated when the locals entered public places. Gunplay was becoming common and the town's undertaker was becoming the busiest man in town.

Sam returned the pair of hired horses to Anvil. The huge man was firing his furnace with a pair of bellows. He looked up, anticipating business, and frowned, rather disgruntled at Sam. 'Brought 'em back have you, at long last?' And he plunged the U-shaped metal into the water-trough, its hissing sound reminiscent of beans hitting the frying-pan.

'I have, and I'm sorry for keeping them so long, but I've lived a whole lifetime since I saw you last.' Sam Cotter's handsome face had seemingly aged in Anvil's eyes.

'So I've heard, and there's going to be more trouble if what I hear tell is right.' The blacksmith's face clouded over again.

'Are you saying Sully's back in town?' Sam demanded grimly.

'He and Hoot Clackson are running Hometown and if you show your face, they'll hang you for Poker Dines' death.'

'I didn't kill the deputy,' Sam protested.

'Maybe you did and maybe you didn't and no one's going to worry about the dead son-of-a-bitch, but that won't stop them coming for you.'

'Can I bed down here for the night?'

'Suit yourself, but I want you gone at first light.'

Sam and the troopers managed to make themselves scarce in the upper

248

loft of the smithy, feeding themselves on the hardtack from their saddle-bags, but hardly had darkness fallen, when Sam felt the barrel of a shot-gun in his face.

'Wake those soldiers up and you'll die now,' whispered a voice that sounded slightly familiar, as Sam was dragged down the loft-stairs and bundled on to a waiting horse.

In very little time, Sam found himself amongst the carousing locals in The Centre, the scantily clad girls dragging at his trousers as he was lugged upstairs to face the clan. Quickly he was slung on to a chair by a burly, unshaven wretch, whom he saw was one of the men who'd assaulted Dee down by the river near Camp Waterfall.

'You'd better believe it's me,' said Max, seeing Sam's immediate sign of recognition.

'I told you my turn would come,' said another, as Sam raised his head and recognized the hunched form of Sheriff Sully leaning back in his chair, his feet stretched over the table, to the obvious discomfort of the pig-faced Hoot Clackson.

'What are you going to do with this man?' Clackson's sunken eyes betrayed the fear of a man who'd lost control.

'He's a dead man, Hoot, and you ought to be glad. You did after all, pay young Ben Wild to kill his friend, Chip Ross.' Sully grinned at Sam, before taking another slug from the whisky bottle lying on the table.

'Take it easy with that stuff. You won't think straight.' Clackson's voice betrayed his pent-up anger, his dreams of a fortune disappearing before his eyes.

'I'm thinking properly, Hoot. You've made all the money whilst I've done the dirty work. Now it's our turn.' The sheriff looked around at his gunslinging friends who grinned and nodded with approval.

'There's plenty to go round. The railway surveyors have arrived and it's only a question of time before Chip

Ross is relieved of his land. Let's not have any unnecessary gun play,' suggested Clackson, nervously.

'There's no problem, Hoot. I've decided that as the leader of this outfit, my share of the gambling receipts will now be twenty-five percent and I'll run the girls,' said Sully sitting up in his chair, assuming his authority.

'Whatever you say Rick. It sounds OK to me.'

'Of course it does. You don't care who dies for your greed.'

'I've killed no one.' Hoot almost spilt the whisky as his hands shook the bottle, nervously.

'You don't kill anyone. You just have it arranged,' said Sully, slyly eyeing his one-time boss.

'I'll have you know I'm a law-abiding citizen and a magistrate.'

'But you nearly started an Indian war with the cavalry,' Sully replied.

'I don't know what you're talking about. The Army were responsible for the slaughter. They were doing their job.'

'With the help of a little blackmail.'

'If you keep on with this nonsense, I'll have the county marshal over. He'll clear my name,' said Clackson as he got up off his chair. He staggered across the room, his right hand edging towards the inside of his hideskin jacket.

'I wouldn't do that Hoot. There are too many guns.' Sully signalled for one of his men to grab the rich landowner who was unceremoniously bundled on to a quilted sofa.

'Let's get rid of him now, boss,' said Butch, evilly watching the landowner who was sitting, moodily wondering how to extricate himself from the unexpected situation.

'You and Max have caused enough trouble with the Miller woman, so just shut up and let me think.' Sully stared across at Sam, the latter holding the sheriff's eye and not flinching.

'What are you going to do with me?' Sam ventured, comprehending he was the real problem.

'I could ask you to throw your lot in

with us, but you can't use a gun and one or two of the boys have you in their sights.' Sully winked at Max and Butch whose memory of their fight over Dee was very fresh.

'I can ride any horse,' Sam said, playing for time.

'That won't save your hide,' snarled Butch, his hand fingering the trigger of one of his Colt revolvers.

'I want all of the boys back at the hideout, before I deal with the railway people,' Sully said suddenly, thinking about the land deal Clackson had set up.

'And I'll handle the soldiers,' Hoot Clackson intervened, seeing his chance of a re-entry into the proceedings.

'You'll shut up and do as you're told,' Sully responded, standing up and moving towards the door.

'Let's do the town, boss, and have fun with the girls first,' suggested Max, angrily waving a revolver in the air and firing a slug into the ceiling, an action that brought all the gunmen to their feet, their cheers causing Sully to draw his large, Army revolver from its holster.

'I'll kill the next man who misbehaves,' he said, pinning the sheriff's badge to his coat.

'I thought you'd finished with all that law stuff,' beamed Clackson, beginning to sense the ex-lawman had changed his mind. But he needn't have worried for the door to the room suddenly flew open and in the doorway stood the strapping figure of Chip Ross, his penetrating brown eyes having lost their pleasant appeal and his hands hanging loosely close to his holsters.

'Over here Sam,' the ranch owner shouted and he threw a shot-gun at his erstwhile partner, whose athletic build enabled him to grasp it with ease.

'Am I glad to see you!' Sam said, his face a picture of relief as he hustled forward towards the door. Suddenly he fell into a heap as a shot rang out, followed by three others. The room filled with the fumes and smell of gunpowder.

'Can you get to your feet?' Chip cried anxiously, both guns drawn and pointing at the ashen-faced outlaws, the gunmen standing, menacingly, close by.

'I think so,' answered Sam feebly, clutching his left shoulder, a bullet having struck him from the back and just above the heart. The blood was seeping through his fingers and his wan face drawn with pain.

'Sit on this chair!' Chip, using his foreleg, hooked it across to where Sam was forcing his back against the open door, his legs wedged against the opposite doorframe in an effort to rise. Eventually, he managed to clamber on to the chair, his attempt having drained all his strength, the shot-gun lying across his lap.

Through his barely open, sunken eyes, Sam saw that Hoot Clackson lay crumpled on his side, at the foot of the couch he had once occupied, another body of a gunman slumped across the crooked table, together with another colleague sprawled, face down, across two shattered chairs.

'What happened?' he asked weakly.

'You owe your life to Sheriff Sully. He plugged Hoot Clackson before he could get another shot in,' Chip answered, 'and I managed those two we came across the night they attacked Dee.' Chip smiled with gruesome satisfaction.

'I guess I should thank you, Rick,' said Sam and then suddenly slumped forward.

'Send for Doc Turner,' screamed Chip down the stairs through the open doorway, the crowd of revellers and their girls stunned into sobriety by the gunplay. One of the bystanders yelled the doctor's name as he flew through the swing doors of the bawdy saloon.

'I guess I owe you that one for framing Nickel Joe,' apologized the lawman, 'but it wasn't my idea.' He held his guns at the ready and in the direction of his one time companions. Chip busily tried to stem the blood flowing from Sam Cotter's fearsome wound.

Soon the doc arrived and ordered the onlookers to carry the lanky young Englishman downstairs, the saloon having been cleared for the attempted, life-saving operation.

'Look after him, Doc. He's a great horseman and my pardner,' shouted Chip, grimly, closing the upstairs door.

Viewing the surroundings with obvious distaste, Chip dragged the body of Hoot Clackson into a decent, sombre position, feeling sorry for the dead man, despite the man's greed for his land.

'What do we do with the other live ones?' queried Chip, staring at the gunmen who stood, edgily, whilst Rick Sully held them at bay.

'You're now sworn in as my deputy and we'll march them off to jail,' said Sully, relishing his change of mind.

'But I thought you were with the gunslingers?'

'It crossed my mind; but I only like straight badmen and neither Clackson nor the others could be trusted. I've seen too many innocent settlers killed by Indians on the warpath and most of it caused by greedy landowners.'

Soon Chip and the lawman hustled the remaining six gunmen towards the jail, intending to lock them up overnight with their release the following morning dependent on their agreement to leave Hometown for good. Chip's concern was more for the health of his friend, Sam, than for the welfare of the unruly mob that thought it ran the fast-growing settlement.

'How's he doing Doc?' cried Chip as he left the saloon.

'I've managed to remove the lead and stop the bleeding,' the doctor answered, his face covered in sweat.

'Check those dead bodies upstairs, when you've finished, and send for the undertaker,' shouted Sully, as he and his new-found deputy disappeared with their charges.

★　★　★

'I was really worried when you disappeared several days ago,' said Dee. Her blue eyes sparkled as she clung to Chip's arm and her beautiful, childlike complexion was a wondrous contrast to the way she'd looked when she had discovered her boyfriend had suddenly decided to ride off after Sam Cotter.

'I had it all worked out, but I couldn't tell you,' said the rancher, smiling happily at the girl he'd secretly admired for years.

'But I didn't know where you'd gone. I thought perhaps you'd been carried off by Sully and his cut-throats,' said Dee, reliving the past with a frown.

'I was in no danger, but I had to stay out of Sam's sight and not let him believe he was being followed. He had to return the horses, otherwise he would have been arrested and made to face the consequences. I knew he'd be headed for trouble as soon as he was spotted in Hometown.'

'I'm glad to know he's getting better.' Dee watched the soldiers heading off the land and across to Hoot Clackson's spread, the young lieutentant having survived the flu, with the help of Gentle Sunrise.

Whilst Chip had been rescuing Sam, the officer had busied himself with over-seeing the clearing of Camp Waterfall and the security of the adjoining ranches, in anticipation of the railway surveyors' arrival. The remaining sick and wounded troopers were nursed back to health by Gentle Sunrise. The lieutenant's foresight was well founded, for the sheriff's change of mind had enabled Chip to despatch Sam's original soldier escort back to his ranch, announcing the arrival of the govern-ment agents and railway people.

Sully's resumption of power, together with his former restriction on the carrying of firearms, had calmed the town. The prospect of work with the new railway company assisted the soothing effect.

'I'm so pleased Sam's going to be all right,' said Dee as she turned towards

Chip, her tenderness and spontaneity allowing her arms to fold about his neck.

'He had a narrow escape. If Clackson's gun had been a forty-five, he'd 'ave been dead.'

'I've never seen him with a gun.' Dee's face registered surprise.

'He had a small handgun inside his skin-jacket. I think it's one of the reasons Sully turned against him.'

'It's a good thing he's a bad shot,' said Dee.

'It was. He was aiming at me!' At Chip's words Dee Miller hugged him very tightly, her past stupidity and stubbornness over her previous desire having disappeared.

'But what about the Crow women and children?' Dee's change of heart over the Indian people had really brought out Chip's love for his long-time fancy.

'I'll take them across the Rockies towards the buffalo and eventually to another one of their families.'

He looked sad at the thought of losing such good, trusty friends.

'And what will we do?'

'You and I'll settle down together, with Sam as a pardner.'

'But the railway's coming . . . and perhaps I don't want to get married,' Dee said coyly.

'I'll have enough money from the sale of my land to buy another spread in California and raise horses, but if you don't like the thought . . . '

'Just try and go without me.' Dee kissed her intended violently, her love and joy obvious.

THE END

We do hope that you have enjoyed reading this large print book.

Did you know that all of our titles are available for purchase?

We publish a wide range of high quality large print books including:
Romances, Mysteries, Classics
General Fiction
Non Fiction and Westerns

Special interest titles available in large print are:
The Little Oxford Dictionary
Music Book, Song Book
Hymn Book, Service Book

Also available from us courtesy of Oxford University Press:
Young Readers' Dictionary
(large print edition)
Young Readers' Thesaurus
(large print edition)

For further information or a free brochure, please contact us at:
Ulverscroft Large Print Books Ltd.,
The Green, Bradgate Road, Anstey,
Leicester, LE7 7FU, England.
Tel: (00 44) **0116 236 4325**
Fax: (00 44) **0116 234 0205**

A TOWN CALLED
TROUBLESOME

John Dyson

Matt Matthews had carved his ranch out of the wild Wyoming frontier. But he had his troubles. The big blow of '86 was catastrophic, with dead beeves littering the plains, and the oncoming winter presaged worse. On top of this, a gang of desperadoes had moved into the Snake River valley, killing, raping and rustling. All Matt can do is to take on the killers single-handed. But will he escape the hail of lead?

RODEO RENEGADE

Ty Kirwan

When English couple Rufus and Nancy Medford inherit a ranch in New Mexico, they find the majority of their neighbours are hostile to strangers. Befriended by only one rancher, and plagued by rustlers, the thought of returning to England is tempting, but needing to prove himself, Rufus is coached as a fighter by a circus sharp shooter, the mysterious Ghost of the Cimarron. But will this be enough to overcome the frightening odds against him?

GAMBLER'S BULLETS

Robert Lane

The conquering of the American west threw up men with all the virtues and vices. The men of vision, ready to work hard to build a better life, were in the majority. But there were also workshy gamblers, robbers and killers. Amongst these ne'er-do-wells were Melvyn Revett, Trevor Younis and Wilf Murray. But two determined men — Curtis Tyson and Neville Gough — took to the trail, and not until their last bullets were spent would they give up the fight against the lawless trio.